CRESCENT STAR

CRESCENT STAR

NICHOLAS MAES

A NOVEL

DUNDURN PRESS

TORONTO

Project Editor: Michael Carroll
Editor: Nicole Chaplin
Design: Jennifer Scott
Printer: Webcom

Library and Archives Canada Cataloguing in Publication

Maes, Nicholas, 1960-
　　Crescent star / by Nicholas Maes.

Issued also in an electronic format.
ISBN 1-55488-797-6.--ISBN 978-1-55488-797-2

　　I. Title.

PS8626.A37C74 2011　　　jC813'.6　　　C2010-902670-5

1　2　3　4　5　　　15　14　13　12　11

  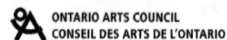

Conseil des Arts du Canada　Canada Council for the Arts

Canada

ONTARIO ARTS COUNCIL
CONSEIL DES ARTS DE L'ONTARIO

We acknowledge the support of the **Canada Council for the Arts** and the **Ontario Arts Council** for our publishing program. We also acknowledge the financial support of the **Government of Canada** through the **Canada Book Fund** and **Livres Canada Books**, and the **Government of Ontario** through the **Ontario Book Publishers Tax Credit** program, and the **Ontario Media Development Corporation**.

Care has been taken to trace the ownership of copyright material used in this book. The author and the publisher welcome any information enabling them to rectify any references or credits in subsequent editions.

J. Kirk Howard, President

www.dundurn.com

Dundurn Press
3 Church Street, Suite 500
Toronto, Ontario, Canada
M5E 1M2

Gazelle Book Services Limited
White Cross Mills
High Town, Lancaster, England
LA1 4XS

Dundurn Press
2250 Military Road
Tonawanda, NY
U.S.A. 14150

ACKNOWLEDGMENTS

I would like to thank Michael Carroll for both suggesting that I write a book about Israel and being so open to the central argument of *Crescent Star*. If, as I say in the introduction, I am standing in the middle of a highway with trucks rushing by in both directions, he is the driver who stopped and kindly offered me a ride. I would also like to thank Nicole Chaplin for her strong critical eye and tireless efforts: the text is much improved because of her.

INTRODUCTION

The Israeli-Arab conflict has lasted over a hundred years, and spanned my lifetime and then some. It has been described, reported on, filmed, analyzed, and exploited a million times over. How odd that a nation smaller than Vancouver Island (or the same size as the state of New Jersey), with a population of 7.5 million (6 million Jews, 1.5 million Arabs), should trigger such scrutiny, obsession, and heated emotions, at the expense (all too often) of other tragedies across the globe, many much more problematic than these Middle Eastern "troubles."

When I told my family and friends that I was going to write a novel about Arab-Israeli relations they thought I was crazy. What on earth could I add that was new to the dispute? Didn't I know that half my readers would only condemn me? Any tale that painted Israel in an attractive light would be poison in the eyes of its many critics; and any sympathy shown to the Palestinians would only stir up a hornet's nest of neocons and Zionists. And to recount events "even-handedly," to create a tale in which Jews and Arabs somehow come to understand each other, would be to deny the hard reality of the conflict and to indulge in fantasies. There was nothing to be gained, except embarrassment and tears.

So what did I hope to accomplish with *Crescent Star*? Having observed this conflict for the last thirty years (mostly from afar but at times from close up) I confess I have no unique wisdom to offer. If asked to propose a solution, I could do no better than the usual platitudes: the two sides have to compromise, respect each other, beat their weapons into ploughshares, etc.

On the other hand, I would like to think that *Crescent Star* does justice to the complications that plague daily life in Israel and which both populations must somehow come to grips with. The novel is descriptive more than anything else, and might possibly serve as an antidote to those who recklessly pass judgment on the players involved. This is not to say that condemnation is always misplaced. The Israeli involvement in Sabra and Shatila was shameful (as most

Israelis would readily admit); and the Palestinian suicide bombings are morally indefensible and barbaric. I start with the general assumption, however, that there is good reason for the Israelis to treat the world with suspicion, and good reason for the Palestinians to resent the Israelis.

Here's an example of what I mean. From a centrist Israeli point of view, the construction of the recent "defense perimeter" is an elegant solution to a horrifying problem: how does one stop repeated suicide bombings? If this same "apartheid" wall is viewed from the Palestinian perspective, it is yet another means by which the authorities control their Arab subjects. To agree with the Jewish conclusion — that the fence as it stands at present is the perfect solution to terrorist attacks — is to ignore the near paralysis it causes innocent Palestinians. To insist this same fence is an abomination and serves no use but to bully a helpless population, is to close one's eyes to the horrific bombings and the right of a nation to protect its citizens.

Whereas most commentators discuss the wall with the goal of getting readers to agree with their conception of it, *Crescent Star* asks its readers to consider and evaluate both perspectives. A character might be leading readers to conclude the wall is a sound proposition, only to have someone else yank them back and argue an entirely different position. And what is true of the wall is true of other contentious issues.

Some readers will undoubtedly feel that, because I haven't come out openly and beaten Israel with a critical club, *Crescent Star* is a manifestation of the usual Zionist shtick. Others will leap to the conclusion that, because I describe some events from an Arab perspective, I am either anti-Zionist or a shameless moral relativist. It is just as my friends warned me: trucks are roaring by in both directions and I am stupidly standing in the middle of the road.

I suppose my only answer is that if both groups are convinced that I have betrayed their cause, then I have achieved my objective. If I seem both anti-Zionist and anti-Palestinian (or, more positively, pro-Zionist and pro-Palestinian) then my narrative has perhaps captured the maddening complexity of daily life in the region. I would like to think that I have not papered over these complexities nor "seduced" readers into thinking what I want them to think. Instead if they are confused and infuriated as the story unfolds then I have been true to the feelings on both sides of the equation and have done a good job of capturing aspects of the Israeli-Palestinian narrative.

Let me end with an attempt to answer my would-be critics with two generalizations. For those who feel I am too soft on Israel, I strongly suspect peace will only arrive in the region when a Palestinian state eventually comes into being, fully autonomous and separate from Israel. At the same time (for those who contend I am anti-Zionist), if such a state does appear on the map, I suspect it will be successful (in the Western sense of the word) if, and only if, it follows the Jewish state's example; that it is to say, if it grants its citizens inalienable rights, is accountable for its actions, and invests in the same services and infrastructure that have rendered Israel a truly open, progressive, and wondrous nation in its sixty odd years of existence.

It is all too easy to condemn the region outright. To understand it, or at least to attempt to do so, is surely the first step one must take on the long, arduous path to virtue.

CHAPTER ONE

The rain kept falling. Water was dripping against each surface in Jerusalem: the houses, the stores, the cafés and cinemas, the cars and buses, the city's famed monuments, layer upon layer of foundations and walls that, over thirty centuries, had witnessed miracles and bloodshed. Jews, Christians, Muslims, and atheists, the rain struck them all alike, indifferent to their disparate outlooks. This was the *malkosh*, the last storm of the spring. It was a pity rain was so infrequent: it was the one, sole blessing everyone could agree on.

At the foot of one building dating back three generations, a cat was scavenging in a garbage bin. It could smell chicken bones and was frantic to retrieve them. Attacking a plastic bag with its claws, it was oblivious to the rain, the odd passing car, and, at the end of the street, the city's old district: Suleiman's walls stood a short distance off. Absorbed with the prospect of a lavish feast, the cat didn't care that it was straddling two realms, one Jewish, one Arab, each apprehensive of the other. Politics meant nothing when food was at stake.

Almost there, the smell of grease was tantalizing. A few more strokes and …

The cat froze. Something had fallen and landed near its whiskers. It was small, cylindrical and … *Ouch!* It burned. The cat eyed the smouldering object until it fizzled in the rain. Wrinkling its nose, it returned to the food.

"You're smoking another?" Avi Greenbaum asked, his brown eyes opened wide in surprise. He and his brother were on a porch above the street. Their mother was visible inside their apartment, clearing away the cake she'd baked to celebrate Avi's fifteenth birthday. The TV was on; it was almost time for the news.

"Leave me alone," Dan grumbled, lighting up a cigarette, "I hear enough from *Ima* about my smoking." He inhaled, held the smoke in his lungs, and blew it out contentedly. "Every soldier in my unit smokes a pack each day. The captain goes through two packs. Our colonel's worse and smokes nonstop; I'd say he's up to four packs now. And the general must smoke six, which means the prime minister goes through cartons. I sure would hate to see the state of his lungs."

He smiled as he took a drag, his lean frame huddled against the chilly air. Avi nodded. His brother always smoked when he'd had a rough day. Dan was attached to a military unit that policed the barrier in the Jerusalem region, and he'd seen more than his fair share of trouble. And because he'd been promoted to lieutenant last month, his decisions affected the people around him, himself, his buddies, and the wider population — Arabs and Jews. Studying his brother's sharply drawn features, Avi thought he was entitled to smoke.

"So what do you think?" Dan asked.

"Of Dror?"

"Who else?"

"He seems okay. He's arrogant, like most *kibbutzniks*, but very smart. I also like that he's into jazz: it says a lot in his favour. I still can't believe Rachel's getting married. And you? What do think?"

"He's seems decent. I'm surprised she fell for a techno geek. I saw her marrying the poet type, you know, someone who works for Tnuva cheese and writes poems about children praying as tanks roar by.… His floating eye would drive me crazy."

"It makes him look shifty," Avi agreed, "like a zombie in a bad horror movie."

His brother laughed and Avi almost glowed. Dan was older by only five years, but he often acted a lot like a father; since their dad's return to Toronto four years back, Dan had tried to fill his role. Because he'd picked up Hebrew quickly and adapted to Israeli ways at school, he'd helped their mom with the stuff their dad should have seen to: the mortgage, insurance, and other such details. Rachel was the oldest but they relied on Dan.

His father. That reminded him.

"*Abba* hasn't phoned. Do you think he forgot?"

"That it's your birthday? Nah. He always remembers. He'll phone soon, I guarantee."

"It's too bad he couldn't come for *Pesach*."

"His work keeps him busy. It wasn't his fault."

Dan said this firmly. He hated even the slightest hint that their father had been wrong to go back to Toronto. The way he saw it, their dad had wanted to stay but hadn't been able to earn a good living. By returning to Toronto and his job as a lawyer, he could pay the family's expenses and keep them on in Israel. So he was self-sacrificing, not a failure or quitter. Avi had his own take on his dad's decision, but it wasn't one he could share with Dan, unless he wanted a yelling match.

"*Ima* was crying when she served the cake," he said, steering the talk to safer ground, "Sometimes she's too sentimental."

"You're turning fifteen," Dan said. "Your childhood has ended."

"I thought that happens at thirteen for us Jews."

"You know what I mean. You're filling out. In another three years' time you'll be entering *Tzahal*. Your teachers will treat you differently now, they'll show you new stuff and get you ready for the army. You'll even learn how to handle a gun."

Avi nodded. It made him faintly nauseous to think that soon he too would be part of the army. And Dan was right: the "grooming" had started. Their phys. ed. teacher had been yelling all year that they had to be in top condition; in geography they were learning to use a map and compass. And teachers were discussing their army service, in low, serious tones, the way one would engage men, not adolescents.

He had to keep his hands from shaking.

"I love this rain," Dan said, flicking a butt into the air, "but we should go in before Dror thinks we're avoiding his eye."

Putting his arm around his brother, Dan steered him inside. Although the apartment was small and cold in winter and the plumbing was faulty, it was a cozy space overall. The furniture was comfortable, and there were shelves with books on all kinds of subjects. The walls were covered with gorgeous landscapes that

Avi's mother Shosh had painted. Many depicted winter scenes: Shosh was convinced they would cool things down in summer, if only psychologically. The TV stood against one wall; Rachel and Shosh were watching the news, along with Rachel's fiancé Dror.

"There was an incident by the wall," Dror said. A muscular guy, he was dressed in jeans and a T-shirt stamped with the smiling image of Bob Marley. He was warm and friendly and spoke with self-assurance, as if he knew better than everyone else — a typical Israeli. "They say a couple of shots were fired."

"There was an incident," Dan spoke tartly. He didn't like discussing the day's events, in case the wrong emotions were provoked. "It happened at the Kalandiyah checkpoint. There was a family with a very sick child — he had leukemia and needed a blood transfusion. They had to get to a hospital fast but lacked the right permit and begged the guard to let them pass."

"So what happened?" Rachel asked. With her chestnut hair and bony features, she looked the spitting image of Dan. "I'll bet the guard didn't lift a finger."

"He had his orders," Dan replied. "And you have to remember the lineups are huge. Everyone's on edge, the guards and civilians."

"How did it end?" Shosh was eyeing Dan. His stories

always drew her in, since they gave her an insight into events that would otherwise pass unseen.

"The father got so angry that he threw a punch. He was quickly subdued but other Arabs moved in and three warning shots were fired. I arrived five minutes later. We called an ambulance and let the boy through. As soon as he was gone, the crowd calmed down. The father's being detained, but he should get off with a warning."

"Those checkpoints are monstrous," Rachel cried. "Those concrete towers are soul-destroying, not to mention the turnstiles and walls of steel. We treat the Arabs no better than cattle."

"What about that bomb last week?" Shosh interjected, "It killed nine people in Tel Aviv and injured dozens more. Without the wall I couldn't sleep at night. I know it's not perfect, but I'm glad it's there."

"That's why we're pushing a million Arabs around? So that you can sleep soundly at night...?"

The debate raged on. Although the women appealed to Dan and Dror, the men kept their distance. It was always like this: while the men might argue among themselves, they seldom spoke their minds when women were present. Avi suspected they knew things that the women weren't exposed to: facts and hard-won information that would pull the plug on any such discussion.

As always, he had nothing to say. He'd heard them argue so many times before that there wasn't anything new to add. And their talk made him very uneasy, especially because he'd turned fifteen. Something was over, something precious was gone. It had been slipping for the last three years but, as Dan himself had hinted, it had disappeared completely that day. The age fifteen seemed to make all the difference. The old Avi Greenbaum, who built forts out of pillows, who played with Lego for hours on end, who constructed model planes and watched hours of cartoons, this Avi Greenbaum was a thing of the past.

Who would replace him?

"Enough politics," Dror finally broke in. "Let's discuss something else, like where we'll live after we get married. Rachel wants to stay here, but I would like to live in Tel Aviv."

"Why would you want to live in Tel Aviv?" Shosh asked. "It's full of crazy drivers."

"As opposed to Jerusalem where people are nuts with religion," Dan observed.

"Exactly," Dror agreed. "I would like to live somewhere normal for once."

"Then you'll have to leave the country!" Dan joked.

"We're not moving from Jerusalem," Rachel insisted, "I want to be able to walk to the *Kotel*."

"But you never go to the *Kotel*!"

"That doesn't matter. It makes me feel safe to know it's nearby."

"I know what you mean," Shosh said approvingly. "It makes me feel secure as well…."

These comments led a new discussion about the value of sticking to the old traditions even if you weren't that religious. Avi had heard these arguments too and found them just as tedious. Why couldn't they discuss something positive, like music? Thank God the telephone intruded just then. And he guessed who it was before he picked up the receiver. His dad had remembered, as Dan had promised he would.

"Happy birthday, Avi."

"So you did remember!"

"Have I ever forgotten? My keys I forget, or my secretary's name, but birthdays, never. What's it like to be fifteen?"

"It's the same as being fourteen but I get to stay up later." If only it were as simple as that. "I'm sorry you're not here. We missed you at *Pesach*."

"Things didn't work out. It's too bad too because the weather has been awful. It's snowing here, even as I speak. We had a blizzard last week and it's storming again. Why people ever settled here is way beyond me."

As he went on to say he would be there for the wedding, Avi pictured him in his downtown condo, with snow burying the city alive, and the traffic on Yonge Street brought to a standstill. Every tree would be coated in white, the city's sounds would be beautifully muted, and everything would move in slow motion. He realized with a pang that he missed the winter. Far from being inconvenient, the snow was padding against the … crap out there. And his father knew as much. As sorry as he was to live far away, Avi could hear his relief even as he complained.

Why was he relieved? For the same reason Avi regretted that he'd turned fifteen.

"… Are you going to that music festival in England?"

"As far as I know," Avi said, returning to the conversation. "We were told to have a valid passport ready. That means it's still on."

"Great. And have you opened your present?"

"I have. Thanks a million. The Artie Shaw music book was just what I wanted."

"Use it well. Your mom emailed me that you'll be playing soccer against an Arab team. Is that true?"

"Yeah. Our first match starts in a couple of days."

"I ask because I ran into a friend last week. Do you remember Phil Matthews? He's a freelance reporter?"

"I don't think so."

"Well, he's looking for a story with a Jewish-Arab angle. I mentioned something about your match and he'd like to interview a player from each team. Interested?"

"I guess."

"Great. I'll tell him. Now pass me to your mother. And remember: you'll see me in just under four weeks."

Bidding him goodbye, Avi handed the phone over. For a moment he felt an emptiness engulf him. It was the thought of his dad living far away, and his brother's fatigue, and the news on TV, and the fact another year had passed, and soon, very soon, he would have to do what all men do. He closed his eyes. The feeling wouldn't pass. To stabilize himself, he sat next to Dan who, sensing his mood, passed some pistachios over.

"How's *Abba*?" he asked.

"The same. It's snowing in Toronto."

"I'd love to see it snow," Dan said.

The siblings began discussing the stuff they missed most in Canada. Between them they mentioned diners, hockey, thunderstorms, forests, lakes, and summer camping. Rachel mentioned the trips they'd taken, and Dan agreed he missed them most, jumping in the car and heading down a highway, to P.E.I., B.C., or south of the border, on and on, seemingly forever.

Dror asked about P.E.I., and Dan and Rachel

clued him in. Still reeling from his empty feeling, Avi grabbed some nuts and passed outside.

It was beautiful out. The rain was like a whisper in his ear. Water was streaming in drops from a drain-pipe and the tempo reminded him of Artie Shaw's "Temptation." Glancing into the street below, he spied a cat clawing around in a dumpster. Thinking it might like a pistachio nut, he cracked one open and tossed it down. It only made the creature jump and, with a growl of suspicion, it ran into the shadows, leaving its cache of chicken behind.

Avi smiled and caught a raindrop on his tongue. He hoped the rain would never let up.

It was 2:00 a.m. when he finally stretched out. His shelves were empty and the walls were bare. His model planes and Lego set had been packed into boxes and stuffed away. He hadn't touched these things in ages but, until that evening, had wanted them around. He still wanted them close at hand but … enough was enough. They had to go. If they weren't staring him in the face each day, it would probably be easier to do what men do.

When he turned the light off in his room, he felt he was saying goodbye to an old trusted friend.

CHAPTER TWO

The rain was tapping against the metal awning. Two potted almond trees were drinking greedily, as if they were knew that this was the last storm of the season. In the distance, merging with the hiss of trickling water, Moussa could hear music playing — the popular song "Habl el-Ghiwa" was coming from a radio. The air was chilly because of the rain and he embraced himself tightly, gazing across the rooftops of the Muslim Quarter. Beyond a network of satellite dishes, solar panels, and stone-cast domes, he could see the outline of the Damascus Gate, its pitted blocks lit up by spotlights from below. Even before the sun began to rise, day labourers would gather at the far side of the gate hoping to be employed by some Israeli; the stalls on Al-Wad Road would open shortly after, and the scent of *sada* coffee would fill the air. At seven, the day would formally begin and the streets would parade the usual roiling crowds, chatting, laughing, and hurling curses at each other.

How many humans had lived in this region, he wondered. Never mind since ancient times, but from the days of Suleiman 400 years back: how many souls had lived in this corner of Jerusalem? A recent census stated there were 26,000 Arabs in the Muslim Quarter. If there'd been an average of 12,000 since Suleiman's day, and if a generation lasted twenty years, the sum of inhabitants was ... 240,000. How impressive for a region that was less than two square miles! And he hadn't considered Mameluke times, Crusader times, Byzantine times, Persian times, Roman times, Maccabean times, Hellenistic times, not to mention the Biblical era. How much food had all these people eaten, how much water had they drunk, how much blood had they spilled...?

"You're buried in thought," Ahmed, Moussa's older brother, said. "Are you playing with your numbers again?"

"I was wondering how much water we've consumed since ancient times."

"Only you would think of such a question. I'll bet you know how many days you've been alive...."

"That's easy," Moussa answered. "Because I turned fifteen today, I've been alive 5,479 days. This includes four leap years since 1991."

"*Ya'allah*, you have an interesting brain." Ahmed lit another cigarette, his fourth since they'd climbed to the roof to rest after supper. Moussa was surprised: Ahmed didn't smoke that often but, when he did, it was because he was feeling cheerful. Had he received good news that day?

"Yes, I'm feeling cheerful," Ahmed said, puffing away.

"You read my mind!" Moussa gasped.

"The logical mind is easy to predict. But you're right. I'm feeling happy. It's your birthday, for one, and I love celebrations. At the same time I'm thinking about Alisha's wedding and how, *insha'Allah*, Douad will be visiting soon. And a delivery arrived so our shelves are full."

"I don't understand. Our shelves aren't always full?"

Ahmed studied Moussa closely. Their father had been arrested two years back when the police had found explosives in a sack of produce, one destined for his dry goods shop. Despite his protests that he was innocent, he'd been tried and sentenced to four years in prison. In his absence, Ahmed had left his studies and taken over the family business. He purchased produce from West Bank farms and sold it from their stall on Al-Wad Road. While Moussa would sometimes help with the deliveries, he didn't show much interest in its details otherwise. This was why he didn't know how the business operated.

"At fourteen you could ignore our hardships," Ahmed said. "But in one short night you have reached the adult realm."

"You're saying I should know why our shelves are sometimes empty?"

"I am. And I'll tell you why. Our supplies arrive from the West Bank and beyond — olives, lentils, peanuts, pistachios, spices, chick peas, and other wares. These goods must be transported into the city, but you can't travel far without encountering a roadblock, manned by teams of Israeli soldiers. These roadblocks consist of concrete blocks, and stop trucks moving in both directions. The only way for the goods to continue is if trucks meet on both sides of the roadblock and the goods from one are loaded onto the other. If the soldiers are suspicious or feeling spiteful, they can turn a truck back before it's been emptied. With nowhere to go, these goods can sit in limbo."

"Does that happen often?"

"More often than it should. And the drivers must have up-to-date permits, there are tariffs to pay, and the timing must be perfect. Many things can go wrong and it's lucky when they don't. And that's why I'm grateful our shelves are full."

Ahmed eyed him. He was waiting for something, but Moussa didn't know what. No, that wasn't true. Ahmed was expecting him to squint his eyes, to clench his fists, and yell something like, "How dare they! How dare they!" The problem was he didn't feel these stirrings. He wished he did; he knew it was time. His teachers expected it, and his friends could often meet these expectations. Most were capable of doing what men do. Hadn't Amir been throwing stones at Israelis and insulting them and spitting as they sidled by? But this fire wasn't in him yet. It would come, he kept thinking; but sometimes he suspected that, when it did arrive, something precious would die, if it hadn't died on him already. Perhaps that was why he had postponed his angry feelings until then.

"Come," Ahmed said, sensing his brother's turmoil. "Let's go downstairs. I could use some coffee."

That said Ahmed flicked his butt into the rain. It flickered briefly and sputtered out. The pair descended a flight of stairs, passed the second level with the family's four bedrooms, and emerged on the ground floor where the smells from dinner lingered still. They entered the living room with its couches and carpets.

The walls paraded an array of pictures — the el-Haram mosque over in Mecca, an official portrait of Chairman Arafat, and three plaques that spelled *Allah* in golden script. Opposite the central couch the TV was playing the news. Alisha and their grandmother were glued to the screen, both identically dressed in *thobes*. At one time Alisha had worn skirts and dresses, but since her engagement she had adopted this traditional style.

"Why are you watching the Israeli news?" Moussa asked. "Your Hebrew is weak. Why not switch to Al Jazeerah?"

"There was an incident at Qalandia. You heard about Nasir?"

"Who's Nasir?"

"Really Moussa! You should know your own family! He's *Um*'s second cousin and lives near Ramallah. His son is sick and needed a doctor. Nasir was rushing him to the al-Makassed Hospital but was held up at the checkpoint. His temper boiled over and he was arrested."

"And his son?"

"*Alhamdulilah*, the Israelis let him pass."

Alisha and Ahmed discussed the event. Both of them were angry. Whereas Ahmed kept shaking his head, Alisha's anger kept growing and growing and she was insisting the soldiers must pay. She even said she wished she were a man, so that she could help in the exaction of justice. When Ahmed joked he couldn't see her with a slingshot, she laughed long and hard, but she was still white with anger.

As always, Moussa moved away, as if he hadn't heard their exchange. He approached his grandmother and grasped her hand. He crouched before her and smiled widely. Her skin sat loosely upon her bones and was so thin the veins in her hands showed through. Always a frail woman, age had reduced her to nothing, as had the arthritis that had plagued her for years. Moussa brought his face in close; her eyes were starting to go as well, and she was practically deaf in one ear.

"Moussa?" she asked, in a voice that sounded like paper rustling.

"*Teita*, it is raining outside."

"I can smell it, *habibi*. It is such a blessing. I remember my brother once dancing in our fields, he was so glad for the rain. That was Mustafa. He would buy me chocolate whenever he could."

"I wish I'd met him."

"I wish you'd met him too. If I close my eyes, I can see him as he was, as if he were dancing in front of me still. Time likes to trick a helpless old woman."

Moussa squeezed her hand. For a moment her wrinkled face relaxed as she indulged this memory from a bygone era. She mentioned it often. It was her happiest one and more precious than gold because her happy memories were all too rare. Moussa smiled and sat in an armchair. He saw Alisha was looking him over.

"You do that often," she said, as if accusing him of something.

"Do what?"

"When bad news is discussed, you walk away?"

"I heard every word you said about Nasir."

"I could have been describing the *foules* at breakfast."

"Alisha has a point," Ahmed said, in a tone that lacked his sister's contempt.

"Sayed says you're old enough to know better," she continued, "and suspects sometimes that you're not patriotic."

Moussa cringed at these words, but he was glad to see that his brother was stung as well. He and Sayed didn't get along: Alisha's fiancé was too pious for his tastes, and Ahmed was too secular for Sayed's pious ways. In the elections that winter, Sayed had supported Hamas. When asked if he didn't find their tactics extreme, he'd said it was their piety that attracted him most. When Ahmed had protested they were strict and violent, Sayed had answered the Gazans needed discipline. Since that conversation, they'd been leery of each other.

"I didn't know," Ahmed spoke, with a note of heavy sarcasm, "that Sayed was such a patriot himself."

"The *shaheed* fight daily to win our freedom! What do you do, besides running your shop? If Moussa doesn't react as he should to our troubles, whom do you think he learned this from? When was the last time you protested? When was the last time you confronted the soldiers, not by counting people's change, but by hitting back with sticks and stones and guns if necessary? And you're surprised he's interested in math and nothing else?"

Moussa wanted to apologize but Ahmed shook his head.

"For reasons of modesty," he said calmly, "you seldom visit the *shuk* these days. This is why you're unaware that many shops have folded, and the rest are like men on the verge of drowning. How do people eat if they can't buy food? How can patriots fight if their stomachs are empty? I have nothing but respect for Sayed, but his prayers won't keep the population fed; nor will the violence that his prayers too often lead to."

"Shame on you, Alisha," Nadira broke in. She was standing with a laden tray of sweets in hand. "Where would Uncle Yusuf be, or your cousins Abdel, Bilaal, and Rashid, if not for Ahmed? Who do you think feeds them when they can't find work or...?"

"*Um!*" Ahmed cried, raising his hand, "You embarrass me. Let's not speak of their troubles but count our blessings. And enough said already. On Moussa's fifteenth birthday we should only smile."

There was silence as Nadira set the tray on a table and started serving the *kanufa* and coffee. Alisha helped her mother, her lips tightly pursed. Moussa was watching his mother's gestures: he was calculating the ways she could pour coffee for five people. He had discovered combinatorics last week and greatly admired this branch of mathematics.

"I'm sorry," Alisha apologized to Ahmed, once he'd sipped his coffee, "I didn't mean to be impatient with you. Please forgive your foolish sister."

"There's nothing to forgive," Ahmed said. "And besides I have good news to announce. I was saving it for when we'd be eating our *kanufa*."

"What news?" Nadira asked. "Does it involve your father?"

"It does indeed. We've received a permit to visit him in jail. We'll see him in two weeks time, on May first."

"We'll have to ride to Beersheva and back in one day."

"We can manage. We'll get up at the crack of dawn."

As the family greeted this news with cheers and discussed the gifts they should bring to their father, Moussa leaned back and tried to join in. Of course he was anxious to visit his father; it had been four months since he'd talked to him last. The problem was, *Ab* would complain like the others, only his words would cut more deeply than theirs. If only the fires would catch inside him. If only he were ready to do what men must do, like his brother or Sayed or his friends at school.

The wind blew a raindrop through the latticed window. Feeling it splash against the back of his neck, Moussa calculated the drops from that day's rainstorm. Even as he reckoned the numbers, he knew the figure would fall short of many tears that his family had shed on behalf of his father.

And still his fires wouldn't catch.

It was 2:00 a.m. when he finally stretched out. His shelves were empty and the walls were bare. His model planes and Meccano set had been packed into boxes and stuffed in a closet. He hadn't touched these things in ages but, until that evening, he had wanted them around. He still wanted them close at hand, but enough was enough: they had to go. If they weren't staring him in the face, it would maybe be easier to do what men do.

When he turned the light off in his room, he felt he was abandoning an old trusted friend.

CHAPTER THREE

Lunging fiercely, Avi stopped the ball. In one continuous sweep of motion, he dispatched it to Izzy who was ten meters off. His kick was hard and accurate.

"Nice shot," Yossi yelled encouragingly. "I see you're feeling mean today."

Avi smiled and wiped the sweat off his brow. Despite the rainstorm three days earlier, the land was parched and the greenery seemed faded. The temperature was high for the end of April and the sun had all the force of a hammer. It didn't help that the soccer field was completely exposed. Still, he loved soccer intensely; it was the only time he knew no fear.

On the edges of the field stood an array of houses, as well as a squat, two storey tower that had been built by the British and should have been razed long ago.

Over in the distance stood the mysterious "hangar," a long, low building whose gates were always closed. Everything was built from Jerusalem stone and, while attractive enough, it intensified the heat.

The ball was coming back at him. It was drifting wide and, with practiced movements, Avi stopped it and prepared to kick it again. But Yossi interrupted. A group of boys was approaching.

"They're here. Okay. Let's gather around."

Nodding, Avi ran over to their coach and waited for the team to assemble. Even in the heat they were a striking sight: their blue shorts and chalk white shirts were bright and fresh and stood out against the parched landscape. Most of them had really filled out. Erez, for example, had been all elbows last year but over the winter had grown some serious muscle. Like all of them he'd been lifting weights, to prepare for the day the army engaged him. After all, the best units required a high fitness level.

"Okay, listen up," Yossi said as soon as everyone had gathered near. "As you know, it has taken my friend Rami and I five months to put this match together. Critics said we were out of our minds, that you guys would end up killing each other. But we persevered. Both of us believe a tournament will draw both sides together. So let's greet our guests warmly and enjoy the game. If things work out, we'll play them again."

Everyone nodded. They had heard that these Palestinians were very skilled and were wondering how well they would fare against them. At the same time they were curious to see some Arabs close up. When Yossi had proposed his idea last December, he'd asked if any of them had talked to Arabs before, not workers on construction sites or cleaners in their buildings, but kids their own age who loved playing soccer. Each of them had acknowledged that, no, they hadn't really talked to Palestinians. They had also laughed self-consciously when they found out that these kids lived minutes away. It was strange, they'd admitted, that a population so nearby could be so removed from their daily radar.

While some had lacked enthusiasm, no one doubted Yossi's motivation. He had served with distinction on the Gaza Strip and been wounded in the course of rescuing someone. He'd been stabbed and his left arm had never recovered. Far from becoming bitter, however, he'd decided to redirect his efforts towards peace.

"But listen," he added. "This is important. Politics has a way of spoiling things, so don't mention topics that will make them angry."

"Like that bombing in Tel Aviv?" Shimshon asked. His cousin had been the victim of a suicide bomber. The young man had escaped with his life but would never be the same.

"That's exactly what I mean," Yossi said. "Look, we can either make this work or all of us can go home now."

"You're right," Shimshon said. "I'll keep my mouth shut."

When everyone had agreed to watch themselves, Yossi ran to greet his friend who was leading the Arab team onto the field. There were thirteen players altogether; their shirts were red and, instead of shorts, they were dressed in matching coal black pants. Some were tall and very solid. Rami was giving them last minute advice.

"Everyone should be on his best behaviour," he said, waving to Yossi who was heading towards them. "I'm tired of watching the news each day and seeing Jews and Arabs kill one another. For once I'd like to be able to say we managed something good between us. A game of soccer might not seem important, but if it's the only peaceful contact we have, it could be more important than anything else. As strange as it seems, you guys are making history."

Moussa looked around. The Damascus Gate was five minutes away but he felt he like he was visiting a foreign country. As soon as you passed through the Damascus Gate, the language was Arabic, the crowds were Muslim, the flag was Palestinian, and the police were your enemy. That wasn't true here: Hebrew was the language spoken, the people were Jewish, and the police, overall, were saints and heroes. He was reminded of the axiom of choice in geometry: in one system parallel lines will never intersect and every proof follows from this basic fact; in another, it's assumed they'll meet and the resulting system is just as consistent. It was amazing such differences could exist side by side.

As they'd walked from their neighbourhood, his friends had muttered strings of insults at the Jews. When they had spotted a cop car, they had spat all together. And they had clenched their fists when three soldiers had passed. Their collective anger was so pointed, in fact, that it seemed to be contributing to the heat. And Moussa? He felt nothing. He swore like them and spat like them, but that vital, angry spark was missing. Happily this would change once he'd started playing soccer. One reason he loved the game was that it triggered the aggression that usually escaped him.

But what was Rami saying?

"... And remember, avoid all talk of politics. We have problems and they have problems. If we dwell on our grievances, it will ruin everything."

"So we shouldn't mention the wall?" Mohammed asked. He had relatives living in a West Bank village. He rarely saw this side of the family because they were never issued the appropriate permits.

"All of us have suffered," Rami said. They knew what he meant. Three years back his brother had been in a riot. The police had opened fire and shot him in the head. Even though it had been a rubber bullet, he died soon after, at the tender age of seventeen. Mohammed nodded and pressed a finger to his lips, his way of signaling he would watch what he said.

Rami smiled and ran ahead. A moment later he and Yossi met: in front of all their students, they openly embraced.

"I'm open! Over here!" Avi cried.

It was fifty-five minutes into the game. The Jews had two points, the Arabs one. Five minutes remained before the match was over — they had agreed to play two thirty minutes halves, instead of the full ninety minutes. The afternoon heat was oppressive but neither team noticed: each wanted to win.

"Erez! Stop clowning. To me or Chaim! He's over on your right!"

NICHOLAS MAES

The Palestinians were very good. Their defense was weak but their strikers were terrific and their over-all conditioning was excellent. Avi's group had played lots of teams in the region but seldom faced such competition. Still, the Israelis were also very strong. Their first goal had been beautiful: Erez had passed to Avi, three meters past the halfway line, and he'd wriggled through two players, finally passing to Chaim, who'd returned it Erez, who'd slipped it to Avi who by then was well within range of the goal. Even before he'd kicked, he'd known he would score. Everything had felt ... integrated. It had come as no surprise when, in a blur of motion, he'd smashed it in, completely catching the keeper off guard.

Why wasn't he fearless like this all the time?

"Chaim! Quick! Back to Erez!"

The other side had scored soon after. The point had come off a corner kick: one player had headed it left of the goal where a teammate had kicked it past Yakovi's left shoulder. The first half had ended a minute after and both sides had eyed each other in ice-cold silence. The coaches had tried to introduce players. After some lukewarm exchanges in broken English these chats had faltered then died altogether. Some smiles were exchanged but the mood wasn't friendly.

42

"No! Watch it! Over on your left!"

Minutes into the second half, the Jews had scored a second goal. Ilan had lobed the ball far forward where, by luck more than anything, Chaim had slipped it in. Not to be outdone, the Arabs scored soon after. Except one player had been off-side — or so it had seemed. The Arabs had cheered, unaware of the error, then fallen into a pregnant silence as the coaches had argued over the goal. "He was off-side I'm pretty sure," Yossi had said. "But maybe I'm wrong." Rami had judged the goal invalid, but his expression was uneasy when his players had groaned.

And now there was only one minute to go. The Arabs had control of the ball and were passing it cautiously back and forth as they sized up the Israeli line for signs of weakness. The ball traveled to a raw-boned teen and Avi dashed forward to intercept it. Even as he caught it with the ball of his foot and pivoted left to avoid the player, he didn't see another kid emerge from behind — Moussa. The pair collided violently. While Avi staggered back from the blow, Moussa was knocked flat.

There was a hush. From down the field, Yossi blew his whistle. Six players were moving in on the scene, three Arabs and three Jews. Their expressions were intense. Avi himself was rubbing his arm and, dazed as he was, could feel his fear wafting back. Steeling himself, he walked over to Moussa.

"Are you okay?" he asked in English.

"*Ha kol beseder*," Moussa answered in Hebrew before continuing in English. "You are very fast."

"So are you," Avi said with a smile. He hesitated briefly then extended his hand. "And I'm sorry I bumped into you. I didn't see you coming."

"It's not your fault. I didn't see you either," Moussa said, a small smile forming on his lips. Then he caught himself. How odd. For the last hour he'd been full of fury and now, because of this collision perhaps, his old tranquility was slipping back. Frowning hard, he brushed off Avi's hand and staggered to his feet.

Sensing the strangeness of the mood at large, the coaches decided to end the game then and there. The Jews had won, 2–1.

The teams shook hands reluctantly, while the coaches kept saying the game had been great and that their teams had never fought so hard. Their smiles were wide, and they meant what they said, but there was something forced about their speech. And when they embraced again, there was something forced about that too, although they agreed the teams should play again on the fifth of May.

Moussa and Avi shook hands as well. They didn't say a word to each other. Avi felt his fear returning; Moussa felt his rage retreating. Each was disappointed in himself. They both joined their respective teams and, within moments, forgot about each other's existence.

The Arab team was back on Al-Wad Road, drinking soda. They were seated a few buildings down from Moussa's family stall and immediately opposite a yawning doorway. If they hadn't been so angry they would have talked about the mystery it posed. Day and night it was watched by a man they called Wasiim (which meant handsome) because he was so unusually ugly. No one knew what lay beyond the door although guesses had been made involving drugs, prostitutes, guns, and magic carpets. But just then they were focused on the game.

"Amir was on side."

"It's typical the Jews would rob us like that."

"And they're violent. Did you see how one of them pushed Moussa over?"

"He pretended he was sorry by offering his hand."

"I'm glad you refused it. The guy was a jerk."

Moussa just smiled. He was thinking, now that the game was over, that the Jew had seemed a decent sort of guy.

Obviously his interior fires had died.

The Israelis were seated outside a *makolet*. They were cooling down with popsicles. They were seated directly across from the hangar whose gates, as always, were firmly closed. If they hadn't been so angry they might have talked about the mystery it posed. No one knew what lay beyond its door, although they'd speculated it was a research centre or a weapons factory or some special kind of jail. They hated the place because it straddled the land that led directly to the soccer field: its closed gates meant they had to trudge three extra blocks to get around it. Their minds weren't on the hangar, but on the soccer match.

"They tried to rob us. That goal was off side."

"That's so typical of Arabs. If they can't win fairly, they'll try to cheat. It's a good thing Yossi was there to keep their coach honest."

"I'm surprised they didn't pick a fight."

"One almost did. Why do you think he knocked into Avi?"

"It was great the way you extended a hand, Avi. You showed him he didn't frighten you one bit."

Avi merely smiled. Now that the game was over and done with, he was amazed he'd had the courage to extend his hand to the Arab.

All his fears had returned.

CHAPTER FOUR

The siren started with a low-pitched sound. It was joined by a high note, then a higher note still, until the tri-tone could be heard across the entire city. As soon as the siren reached their ears, the class stopped chatting and climbed to their feet. The classroom window overlooked a street that was crowded with mid-morning traffic. Every driver had stopped his car, climbed outside, and stood in silence. This same scene was taking place across the nation, in every kibbutz, *moshav*, town, village, city, base, and highway.

As the siren blared — it would last two full minutes — Avi closed his eyes and thought about his *zaidy*. He had died three years earlier and still Avi missed him, especially on occasions like this: his *zaidy* had been a victim of the Holocaust.

He had seldom discussed it. For a long time Avi had assumed his *zaidy* was like other people, despite his accent and foreign habits. At six he had gained some inkling of the truth. *Zaidy* had been over while his parents were out and Avi had asked him, in a fit of curiosity, where all his brothers and sisters had gone. Much to his surprise, his *zaidy*'s brow had darkened and he'd answered in a choking voice, "I had six siblings but Hitler took them." Only later had his mother explained that *Zaidy*'s past had been very hard and some very bad people had destroyed his family.

In later years, of course, he had read about the Holocaust. It was hard to imagine. Six million souls. Much like his *zaidy*, these people had been gentle, loving, decent, and hard-working. It was only because they had all been Jewish — and most never even practiced the religion — that the Germans had sent them to death camps in Europe. And apart from a few exceptional souls, no one had helped. No government, no army, no church, no one.

The spring before his death, *Zaidy* had been in Israel. He and Avi had been standing in a park when the siren had sounded to commemorate the victims of the Holocaust. Avi remembered his strangled expression. His wrinkles had tightened into a grimace of pain as the siren had brought home the losses he'd suffered:

parents lost, siblings lost, aunties, uncles, and cousins lost. Five thousand Jews had lived in his town; by war's end only eighteen had survived. When the siren stopped, the old man had whispered, "They should be here. They should be here. This land is theirs. They should be here."

Avi's eyes opened. Around him his friends were standing at attention, including Dov and Ilan, the two class clowns. They were as serious as everyone else; after all, their families had been gassed as well. Six million people. All that death and sorrow. Pressure mounted behind Avi's eyes and he had to struggle hard to keep himself from crying. His *zaidy*. His poor *zaidy*.

The siren was insistent. "Do you get the point?" it seemed to be screaming. "Do you understand the pain we suffered? Do you understand we must be vigilant always? Do you understand this can't happen again? No nation can ever hurt us again? We can never feel fear again and allow ourselves to be led off to slaughter, like sheep, like goats, like chickens, like cattle? Do you understand? Do you?"

He nodded in silence. He understood. He understood truly.

But still he couldn't shake his fear.

— • —

"So what does the *Shoah* mean today?"

Shulamit, their teacher, was studying the class. Generally good-natured, she was serious for the moment. "Is it is helpful to dwell upon our suffering at length? Certainly we wish to remember the victims, but what do we achieve by reviewing the past? Yes, Ilan?"

"It reminds us that we have to be tough. We were abandoned back in '39. If we were threatened today, the world wouldn't care. So forget about becoming doctors and lawyers. Forget about playing the violin and piano. Forget about business and science and computers. Our survival begins with *Tzahal*. If the Germans had confronted our guys from Golani, they might have thought twice about their Final Solution."

This said, Ilan crossed his arms and stared defiantly at the students around him. His words came as no surprise. His father was part of the Kfir Brigade, which was fighting terrorism across the West Bank. He had addressed the school earlier that year. While decent and good-humoured, he was as tough as they come. And the apple didn't fall far from the tree.

Avi was wondering what type of tree he came from.

"Thank you Ilan. Would anyone like to add something? Dinah."

"Some people say there shouldn't be a Jewish state. They think Israel is prejudiced because it was made with only Jews in mind. But when you think how we were killed in Europe, how every country turned its back on us, we need a Jewish state, if only as a refuge. The gentiles can't be trusted to look after our welfare."

Zohara raised her hand. The students smiled. Her parents were members of *B'Tselem*, an Israeli human rights organization, and were often critical of Israel's tactics. Other students took a liberal line, but Zohara tended to be the most extreme.

"If the *Shoah* taught us anything, it's that violence is evil and counter-productive. Okay, we Jews need a refuge, great, but at what cost to the people around us? I mean, if our country was born from the ashes of the Holocaust, we of all peoples can't behave like Nazis."

The class started shouting when they heard these words. Shulamit whistled. When everyone shut up, she let Zohara continue.

"Do you know what we're up to in the West Bank and Gaza? Every day we smash people's doors and rough them up and throw them in prison. If someone protests, we shoot him dead, not just adults but children too. And for added effect, we demolish their houses. Would any of you want to live in Gaza City? Can you imagine how much filth there is and poverty and sickness? So tell me how we're different from Nazis?"

"Do you really think we're Nazis?" Shulamit asked. "Let's not speak rhetorically. Yes, Aryeh."

"The comparison is disgusting," Aryeh said. "It's true we've sometimes overreacted but even at our worst, we've created nothing like Auschwitz. At Auschwitz a million Jews went up in smoke. As bad as Gaza is — and we all know there are problems — it doesn't come close to an Auschwitz or Belzec."

"I agree that Gaza isn't Auschwitz," Nira spoke — her parents were members of *Shalom Achshav*, an organization dedicated to forging peace. "But Zohara is saying something important. For a population that was treated badly, we tend to use force a little too quickly. It has become a way of life with us."

"But we're usually responding to Arab violence," Ilan cried. "How else can we protect ourselves?"

"If you starve a dog and lock it up, you shouldn't be surprised if it snaps at you. We've created the culture of violence that we're so afraid of." Zohara was on her feet and practically shouting.

"So you're saying the problem lies with us? Every time there's a terrorist attack — and they number in the hundreds and thousands — the fault is always ours? Do you remember Ma'alot, when children were murdered? We were to blame? And the pizza bombing on Yaffa Road? And last week's attack in

Tel Aviv? And what about the first Iraq War, when Saddam launched his missiles on us? Do you remember how the Arabs reacted? They were dancing on their roofs! They were dancing and singing! I could go on but my point is clear. When we resort to violence, we're defending ourselves!" Ilan was standing and waving his arms.

"That's always our excuse!" Zohara sneered. "So tell me, how far should we go to safeguard our survival? Should we lock up everyone? Should we starve and shoot them? We know what it's like to be pushed around. We have no right, in the name of self-defense, to humiliate and arrest and torture and kill. You say we're not like Nazis? Tell that to an Arab whose dad has been shot for no good reason."

"Maybe daddy was a terrorist," Ilan spoke.

"If daddy wasn't," she spat back, "his son will be!"

"But we're still talking hundreds of victims," Aryeh said. "And sometimes they were up to no good. In the case of the Germans, they killed us by the millions, and not because we threatened them, but only because we happened to be Jewish. You can argue we're too rough at times, but to say we're Nazis is total crap."

"And everything's in the open," Itamar spoke. His father was a journalist and wrote for *Ha'Aretz*, "If our troops are rough, it gets reported. My father writes about miscarriages of justice and no one tries to shut him up. Like you, he thinks we sometimes cross the line, but he appreciates the fact our system is so open. He also says the Arab countries don't allow such freedom. Your parents work for *B'Tselem?* There's no such organization in Arab countries. Remember this when you point your finger."

As the discussion rolled on Avi kept silent. The heated exchange was only fanning his fear. In three years he would be armed with a rifle and the decision to kill would be left up to him.

He wasn't ready. He would never be ready.

He glanced at Zohara. He thought she was wrong, but her fearlessness was something. And when she smiled, it was dazzling.

The teacher called for silence. The class would end in thirty seconds and she wanted to end on a decisive note. "All of you should know that we aren't Nazis. Anyone who argues so knows nothing about Auschwitz and nothing about Israel."

Their teacher Ali was standing with his hands behind his back. The wails of the siren were fading at last as the students completed an exercise in Arabic. When the siren died, Ali opened the window and smiled as a breeze rushed into the room. The sounds of the nearby *shuk* intruded, together with the hum of traffic on the move.

"Shall we discuss their tragedy?" he asked the class.

"What tragedy?" Suleiman declared, "My father says the Holocaust is a lot of crap. He says Jews control the media and they spread this lie to hide their crimes against the Arabs."

"My father says they didn't lose six million," Yasser added. "Maybe a few Jews died, but nothing like the numbers they claim."

Before the others could speak, Ali raised a hand. He was short and had a slender build but could control the class using just one finger.

"Why begrudge them their suffering? I have seen the books and movies and pictures. Their *Shoah* did occur and many millions died. But what does that have to do with us? Mahmoud?"

"Okay they suffered," Mahmoud said, slamming his fist against his hand. "But that doesn't mean they're entitled to our land. Why didn't the Europeans pay them off? They could have carved up Germany and let the Jews move there." His family had lost their farm in '48.

"Mahmoud's right," Sami added. "We were never their problem. Their enemy was the Germans and their allies at the time. They should return to Europe and stop plaguing us here." Sami had six brothers. Three were in jail.

"Just because they suffered," Anwar cried, "doesn't mean they get to treat us like dirt. If anything, they should be refraining from violence." Anwar's dad was in the souvenir business. Most tourists had been chased off by the endless strife.

"Not necessarily," Hussein interrupted. "If they suffered in the past, they'll protect themselves in future. In other words, they'll hurt us if we try to rebel. Their Holocaust has made them very tough."

"So we will have to be tougher," Amir said.

Moussa listened as the debate raged on. The number six million was in his head. It was very large and hard to imagine when applied to human suffering. The largest crowd he'd seen had had two thousand people. At Eid-al-Fitr maybe 10,000 people used the old bus station, but that was over twelve full hours. Even pictures from the Hajj involved three million pilgrims and that was only half of six.

He imagined a line of empty desks. Each desk was stationed one meter from the next. If there were a desk for each Jew who'd perished in the *Shoah*, that would mean six thousand kilometers of desks. The image haunted him, of an endless line of wooden tables, extending from Jerusalem to China, say....

"Alright," Ali said, cutting short the discussion, "I think we're all agreed. The Jews suffered badly. And we'll be sure to pity them, once they've given us our own state. Until then, they will only know our anger."

Moussa almost wilted here. When would he feel angry?

CHAPTER FIVE

"The brass section's flat. And I can hear you're slowing down when you play the eighth notes."

Avi shifted restlessly. He hated waiting for the group to catch up. He'd mastered his part of the Mozart Concerto — and his solos were the most difficult segments — so why hadn't everyone mastered theirs? This was why he hated band: one weak player could ruin the whole ensemble. Like Rivka, their conductor, he could hear that Erez was out of tune, Ilana hadn't practiced, and Zohara was off tempo....

"Zohara! On the beat. Dah dah dah now...!"

It was hot in the practice room. Avi's shirt was damp and he was sweating freely. His mind was wandering — never a good sign. They had seen a film about the cell in his biology class. When the announcer had discussed the Golgi apparatus, a trumpet had started sounding in the background. When the film had turned to the mitochondria, a piano had been tinkling away. Why this choice of instruments, he mused? Why did the composer think the mitochondria were best captured by a piano's sounds? And in movies why do violins and cellos reflect sad emotions better than a piccolo, say? And what instrument would capture Avi Greenbaum best?

What instrument best reflected fear?

"Ilana! You've stopped playing! What do you think? Some magical elf will play your oboe for you?"

"But the police are here," Ilana observed. She was sitting by the window and looking outside.

"She's right," Erez said. He had stood up from his chair and joined her by the window. "It's the *chablan mishtara*."

"The *chablan mishtara*?" several students said together. By now everyone was staring outside.

"Let's keep practising!" Rivka cried. When they paid no attention, she looked outside as well.

Two vans were parked in front of the school. They were marked with the Israel Bomb Squad logo and each was fitted with a machine gun turret. Four men in fatigues had blocked off the sidewalks. A fifth man was dressed in an absurdly padded suit and a large, round helmet with a fortified visor. He was using a set of controls to guide some kind of robot. The robot was mounted on caterpillar tracks and equipped with camera lenses, an X-ray sensor, and a metal arm roughly a meter in length. It was drawing near a briefcase that was lying by a tree on the far side of the road.

"It's not a bomb," Rivka grumbled, "but an abandoned bag, that's all.

"I've seen this before, but it's always exciting," Sarah said, glad for the interruption.

"My uncle's in the *Chablan* in Netanya." They had heard Ilan tell this story this a hundred times before. "Last month he and his crew defused a large bomb in the *midrachov*. Can you guess how much damage it might have caused?"

"We should move from the windows," Rivka warned. "If that briefcase is a bomb, the windows could shatter." Avi had been thinking the same, but he hadn't wanted to reveal his fear.

"They would warn us if we were in danger," Erez said. As if he'd been eavesdropping, a soldier glanced up at them and waved them back. They retreated together. Zohara stepped on Avi's foot. He smiled and she smiled back. Seconds later, they had all drifted back to the window. While some of his classmates thought it was one big joke, Avi could picture the entire street in flames.

The robot was by the briefcase and active with its sensors. Its arm was maneuvering to open the latches but either it lacked the dexterity or the briefcase was locked. A voice on a loudspeaker was warning people to keep back. The agents looked surprisingly bored, as if they handled a million such cases before. And most of them had. Every day there were a hundred calls in the city, when bags or parcels were left unattended. Most of the time it came to nothing, but every so often a true threat would arise, with awful results if it weren't properly handled. But the team felt this briefcase was a false alarm.

Again a soldier motioned them back; again they retreated, only to return.

"I'm thinking of joining them when I'm drafted," Ilan said. "Although my dad would prefer I join a fighting unit."

"I'm driving a tank," Itamar said.

"I'm considering the navy," Erez volunteered. "Or intelligence maybe."

"You would have to be intelligent for that!" Ilan joked.

"I'm thinking of intelligence too," Sarah said. "If that doesn't work, I'd join a combat unit."

"A combat unit?" Ilan scoffed. "You can't. You're a girl."

"You're wrong," Rivka answered. "There are several mixed combat units, *Karakel* for example. My sister is a sniper...."

Avi tried to ignore this conversation. It amazed him they could talk so freely about *Tzahal*, without considering the many dangers involved. It wouldn't bother them at all to jump from a plane? To rush into battle? To raid Hezbollah? They couldn't see themselves with broken bones, with blood streaming from a bullet wound, or as a corpse in some barren field, their torso at one end of it, their legs at another? How could they be so lackadaisical? What was the trick...?

An explosion erupted and almost made him jump. The robot had attached two cables to the briefcase and, having backed off a distance, sparked the detonation. There was a burst of smoke and the briefcase shuddered. Its latches burst and the bag caught fire. Charred paper filled the air. The soldiers were disgusted.

A voice on the loudspeaker gave the all clear. Lines of people started moving again as the sappers packed their equipment up. The one with the robot was out of his suit and mopping his brow and gulping water down. For a fleeting second he glanced at Avi. "I just do what men do," he seemed to say, shrugging matter-of-factly.

The students were returning to their music when they heard someone shouting. Glancing outside, they saw a man come running up — the briefcase owner. He looked angry and was gesturing to the ashes on the sidewalk. He was yelling at the soldiers, that he was an important lawyer and they had burned some crucial documents. After letting him rant for all of a minute, an officer swiftly cut him short. Telling the man to shut his mouth, he asked him how he dared complain when, through his own neglect, he had inconvenienced people. The whole class chuckled as the guy slunk off.

They sat and took their instruments in hand. Outside traffic was moving again, people were walking and the "bomb" was forgotten. Everything was back to normal, just like that.

The pictures inside Avi's head were a different story altogether.

Dusk was settling over the *shuk*. The crowds from the day were no longer as dense and the noises too had tapered off: a dove's cooing could be heard in the background. The vendors who were open had turned on their lights and were surrounded by incandescent shells; some were drinking tea and playing *shesh besh* with their neighbours. The smell of falafel hung in the air, as well as *shislik* and a thousand different spices.

Moussa ran his eyes across the stall. Dozens of burlap sacks gaped open and disclosed ground powders of dazzling colour, greens and reds and browns and yellows. Large bags of flour, rice, beans, chick peas, lentils, and other produce were lined up at the back of the stall, within Ahmed's reach so he could process orders swiftly. Bins with nuts stood directly in front and above them hung a scale with a large zinc pan, visible to customers so they could see the weight of goods they'd ordered. The sight was comforting. Not only did this food suggest the family would never suffer from want; the space was one he'd known all his days and was the one steady constant that he could rely on. Ahmed sat behind the counter, his nose buried in a book.

"Are you going to read all evening?" he asked Ahmed.

"We'll lock up soon. And the book is great. It only cost me fifty shekels."

"*The World's Most Famous Buildings Close Up*," Moussa read in English. "Aren't you tired of books on architecture?"

"This one has buildings I've never seen. If I can't visit them in person, the next best thing is to study them in pictures."

"But one building's like another," Moussa said, to tease his brother. "Four walls, a roof, some stairs, a few windows. That's all there is to it."

"Look at this," he opened the book to a photo of the Chrysler Building. "This building is three hundred meters tall, has well over a million bricks and girders, yet it floats on air."

"But it is still just walls and a roof," Moussa said.

"There's more to it than that," Ahmed insisted. "Buildings are so much a part of being human. They reflect our habits and shape our view of the world. Most of us live maybe seventy years and then we vanish; but buildings last forever, the best ones at least."

"Even the largest aren't that strong," Moussa said. He had turned to a snapshot of the World Trade Center.

"*Ya'Allah*," Ahmed cried, with a fleeting look of pain. "That was a terrible day, when these buildings fell. Men who destroy such structures are the enemies of progress."

"Not everyone agrees," Moussa said. "Sayed once said the attackers were heroic."

"That sounds like Sayed," Ahmed didn't bother concealing his scorn. "His anger will get him into trouble one day."

"His anger?" Moussa asked, his interest piqued. "He shouldn't be angry?"

"There are two sorts of anger," Ahmed said. "There is Sayed's kind, that knows only destruction and brought about the evils of 9/11. There is also righteous indignation, which is a natural reaction to unjust dealings. The anger you feel defines the person you are."

Moussa's mouth was open. He was going to ask what Ahmed thought about people who were empty of anger. Before he could he saw two figures approaching. Their details were obscured in shadow but their outlines betrayed them. Ahmed quickly closed his book. He straightened his posture and his face drew closed. Seconds later, the soldiers walked up to the stall.

They were loaded down with equipment. Both were wearing bullet proof vests and blue fatigues with bulging pockets. Each of their belts was strung with a nightstick, revolver, flashlight, handcuffs, and various gadgets. Each brandished a rifle as well, casually slung over a shoulder. They were in their early twenties and looked far from friendly. Their cheeks were clean-shaven, their hair was bristly, and their skin was flawless, as smooth as chrome. Given their equipment and machine-like gestures, they seemed more like robots than flesh and blood humans. One was fair and had bright blue eyes, while his friend was dark and could have passed for an Arab. The fair one was holding a walkie-talkie, from which streamed a voice that was feeding them instructions.

Since their father's arrest two years ago, the cops had often "dropped in" on the Shakirs, along with Shin Bet operatives. Their bags of produce would be thoroughly searched and they were warned that the authorities were always watching, that their every move was being watched. One time the soldiers had caused an awful mess, ripping bags and mixing produce together. When Ahmed had asked if they couldn't be more careful, the officer in charge had told him to be quiet. "If everything had gone according to plan, your father would have killed many people," he'd said. "Just count yourselves lucky we haven't closed your business."

Ahmed cleared his throat and greeted the soldiers. He was sure they were going to ask for his papers, to prove once again that he was under surveillance. Certainly the dark-skinned one was studying his wares, as if inspecting the place for something suspicious.

"Good evening," he spoke in fluent Arabic. "Do you have any cashews? Unsalted ones?"

"Yes. Over here," he replied, motioning to a bin at the far end of a table. "They arrived just yesterday and should be fresh."

"I'll take two hundred grams please."

"Of course. It will be one minute."

"You're reading about buildings," the soldier went

on, motioning to Ahmed's book. "Are you interested in architecture?"

"Very much." Ahmed was filling a bag with nuts.

"Me too. I would like to study it and tour the world's buildings."

"That is my ambition too," Ahmed said with a smile, passing the soldier the bag of nuts. "That will be eight shekels."

"Thanks. Hey Rafi, do you want something?" he asked his partner.

"No. Finish quickly. There's been a stabbing near the Temple Mount."

"Thanks again," the soldier said, stuffing the nuts into a pocket on his hip. "And have a good evening." He hurried in his friend's footsteps, his expression hardening as he wandered off and his hand working the gun off his shoulder.

"He was very nice," Moussa said, once the soldiers were gone. "In a different life maybe you could be friends."

"He is our enemy. We could never be friends. Only a child could think such a thing."

Moussa blushed. He recalled the question he was going to ask, about people who never experience anger. He didn't have to ask it now because Ahmed had already given his answer.

CHAPTER SIX

Avi was with his mom outside a grocery store on Agron Street. He'd wanted to practise his clarinet before the Sabbath began, but she had asked him to help with the shopping. In actual fact, she didn't want to drive by herself. Although it had been five years since she'd gotten her licence, the traffic still made her nervous, not only because it moved very quickly, but because Israelis were impetuous drivers. "Why can't they drive like Canadians?" she would grumble, when people cut her off or honked in irritation. But for some strange reason, when someone was beside her, she could drive as aggressively as anyone else.

"*Shalom giveret*," the store guard greeted them. "Can I look inside your purse?"

"Of course," his mother answered. She opened her purse, allowing the guard to scan its hollows. Avi followed suit with the knapsack on his shoulders. After swiping his pants and jacket with a scanner, the old guy motioned them both inside. "*Shabbat shalom,*" he called to them.

"And to you," his mother replied with a smile.

They moved methodically down each of the aisles. While his mother seemed frazzled at times, as if she'd just arrived in Israel, in her own way she was competent. Her Hebrew was excellent and she'd won herself a government position. She could hold her own with Israelis, many of whom could be difficult at times. And she was tough. Since they'd first set foot in Israel, there'd been attacks and bombings and a near state of war. Through all of these she'd kept her cool, even when she'd missed — by minutes — a bus whose interior had been blown to pieces. To look at her one would never guess that she could handle tension well, unlike his father, a muscular man who, after a single year, had thrown the towel in.

They were moving through the meat section. His mom was excited because the chicken was on sale. As she ordered three kilos of thighs, a friend of hers drew near, another ex-Canadian. They started discussing a friend they had in common, so Avi wandered off and, bored out of his mind, tried composing a song using the brand names around him. As he groped for a word that would rhyme with "Teva," Zohara suddenly rounded a corner, wheeling an overburdened grocery cart. Both of them flinched and she seemed to be blushing. He realized he was blushing, too.

"Hi," he said.

"Hi. I'm shopping," she said, as if he needed to be told.

"I'm shopping too. I'm waiting for my mom who's gabbing with her friend."

"My mother's doing the same!" She had an infectious smile. "She's talking to a colleague. They'll be at it for hours."

"Are they discussing strategies at *B'Tselem*? How to bring the government down?"

"They're discussing a patient who received a bypass — they're colleagues at Shaarei Tzedek hospital."

"I see you're buying Osem products," he observed, motioning to the items in her buggy. "I'm surprised you're still buying Israeli goods. You could probably bring the country down if only you avoided its cookies."

She looked as if she were about to get angry. But, just as suddenly, she chuckled and said, "We're targeting Elite chocolate today. If they go broke, the country will fall."

Both of them laughed. Avi saw his mother was finishing up with her friend. He was going to rejoin her when Zohara called him back.

"Would you like to go for coffee?"

"What? Now? With our mothers in tow?"

"Not now. But maybe next week. We can talk more about bringing the country to its knees."

"Okay. That would be nice."

"Great," she said, "I'll be in touch." As he was moving off, in a near state of shock, she again called out.

"Avi!"

"Yes?"

"You play like an angel."

He returned to his mother who was sorting through the sandwich meat. After observing that he looked very pleased with himself, she said that a friend of hers was moving to Cleveland, having lived in Tel Aviv for six years. "What a waste," she kept saying. "What a terrible pity."

"I guess you're never going back," he said, as they passed into the dairy section.

"Going back where?"

"To Canada. Where else?"

"I would love to see my sister again."

"I mean permanently. After all, you grew up in Toronto. And Dad is there...."

"Look at that. The yogourt is so cheap."

They were strange, his parents. Neither hated the other, even though they had good reason to: his dad because his mom wouldn't leave, or his mom because his dad had bolted. And even though they lived apart, they still seemed very fond of each other. His dad stayed over when he came to visit, and on the phone they were always warm with each other. It was strange that a country had driven them asunder. No, cancel that, it wasn't strange at all. Not when Israel was the country involved, demanding what it did of the people who lived there.

"You haven't answered," he spoke again. "Would you move back permanently?"

"You're like your father," she pretended to groan. "Always cross-examining people. Still, it's a matter of history, I suppose. For centuries we prayed to get back to the Holy Land, for two thousand years that's all we could think of. And then Israel was created — ten short years before I was born. What was I supposed to do? Ignore its existence? So I gave it a shot and, well, I love it here. So no, I'll never leave."

While speaking she'd been placing dairy products in the buggy. Clucking her tongue at the price of the cheddar, she wheeled the buggy to the tinned goods section.

"But everything is harder here," Avi observed. "There are bombs and riots and shootings and wars. In Canada the army wouldn't drag your sons away. And the world loves Canadians whereas it can't stand Israelis...."

"My home is here," she answered firmly, examining cans of tomato sauce. "I have a craving for spaghetti. How about you?"

"Spaghetti would be great."

"And I'll make a Caesar salad. But what about dessert?"

As she moved off to the frozen food section, he followed with the buggy, swallowing hard. Why wasn't he more like her? Why hadn't he acquired her fortitude, instead of his dad's wariness? It was so unjust.

He wheeled the buggy next to her. She was standing in front of a line of freezers and motioning to the ice cream section. Her grin said it all. A country with such an amazing selection of desserts had to be an okay place to live.

From somewhere in the middle of the compound, a heavy metal door slammed closed. The bang started a chain of echoes that bounced down one hall after the next, until the sound reverberated in Moussa's ears. And no sooner had the vibrations died than another door closed, or some bars slammed home, starting the sequence all over again. Since he'd arrived at the prison three hours earlier, there hadn't been one moment of silence. Either the echo of banging metal punctuated the air or ghost-like voices came trickling through, snatches of conversation and lots of cursing. When the language was decipherable, it was Arabic, always. The inmates were Palestinian and doing all the talking, while the guards were Israeli and stone-cold silent. Moussa couldn't decide which group worried him more.

They had traveled to Beersheva on an early morning bus. The vehicle had been crowded and he'd stood all the way, to allow his mother and *jadda* to sit. The drive had taken just over an hour and, while monotonous, had piqued his interest, coming as he did from the heart of the city. Flanking the road were unending fields, all with crops of different kinds, wheat, barley, beans, and sunflowers, which were magnificent as they grinned at them passing. Some fields were covered in plastic sheeting; these conserved moisture, Ahmed had explained. It was no small feat the Jews had managed: they had converted barren desert into fertile fields.

They took a cab from the Beersheva bus station to the prison. The Russian driver, who spoke Hebrew with an accent, knew without asking where they'd wanted to go. While he'd been brusque to the point of hostile, he'd treated their *jadda* with due consideration, being sure to hold her as she entered the cab and to shield her head as she ducked through the doorway.

The jail itself hadn't come as a surprise. Moussa had visited his *ab* before, in different prisons sure, but one was like another. There was always a tower, heavy metal gates, armed guards, and fences topped with razor wire. There was also the tired exercise yard, with concrete walls and mottled dust and a soccer ball whose leather stripping had been patched many times.

The prisoners, too, were always the same. They were mostly adults, about Ahmed's age, although some prisoners were maybe a bit younger than Moussa. They were dressed in jeans, sweatshirts, and sandals and looked as if they hadn't bathed in ages. Many hadn't shaved and looked partially crazed.

And then there were the visitors. They were female, for the most part, and all of them looked worn, with fear and, at the same time, expectation. Unlike the prisoners, who seemed tough as leather, these visitors were sniffling or crying aloud. Many were exhausted. Even if they had the proper permits, many hours could pass before they saw their loved ones. The waiting room where Moussa and his family sat was packed with visitors from across the country, Bethlehem, Nablus, Ramallah, Jenin, each carrying gifts of food and clothing. And cigarettes. Everyone in the prison, guards and inmates alike, smoked like chimneys whenever they could. The air was poisonous, like the compound itself.

"Shakir!" a large guard cried. "Relatives for Tariq Shakir!"

"That's us," Ahmed exclaimed, approaching the guard. Moussa quickly followed as Alisha and his mother helped his *jadda* along. The guard flung back a heavy sliding door and ushered everyone through. Banging the door closed behind them, he led them down a hallway that was glaringly lit with bulbs in wire cages. As Moussa had seen on other occasions, there wasn't one detail to comfort the eye, no paintings, no knick-knacks, no interesting colours. But what he did expect? This place was a jail.

"You have fifteen minutes," the guard announced once he'd led them to a steel cage with a two-foot opening in the grill through which one's hands could be extended. Inside was a pale, thin man with shining eyes and a ragged beard. He was rocking back and forth and smiling widely. He was Tariq, Moussa's father.

"*Ab!*" his children called. For the next two minutes they embraced their father (awkwardly, because the grill interfered), shed some tears, and asked about his health. Assuring them that he was fine, that the food was bland but he was eating well, and that his cellmates were kind and pious men, he looked them over carefully.

He asked how the business was faring. Ahmed swiftly brought him up to date, mentioning the handsome profit that year, who their suppliers were, who owed them money, and who had tried to rob them blind. "Overall we're doing quite well," he concluded. "Especially when you consider the effect of the wall. But we'd be doing much better with you to guide us."

Moussa almost smiled here. When his father had been in charge, he had spent more time exchanging gossip than he had going over the daily accounts. He had also invested his money badly and one year had lost more than fifty thousand shekels. Even with the wall's disruptions, the business had never done so well.

Moussa was also thinking about how his father had been … difficult. At home he'd complained about the frequent mess and his children's flagrant lack of respect. If one of them had laughed too loud, or quarreled with a sibling, or not finished his dinner, Tariq had often lost his cool, and sometimes spanked the guilty party. While Moussa did miss him terribly, he was glad he wasn't there to point out his failings. He sometimes wondered whether his *ab*'s hot temper was somehow responsible for his own lack of anger; but it wasn't right to put this blame on his father.

They were discussing Alisha's wedding now. Tariq said he approved of Sayed. They hadn't met in person yet, but the fact he was religious impressed him greatly. The family could do with a practicing Muslim, unlike his own sons who'd seldom seen the inside of a mosque. An inmate had met Sayed's family, he added, and had only positive things to say. "Men like him will win us a country," he said, "and will gain our family honour in the process. You have chosen well," he told his daughter.

He asked his youngest son how school was going. Moussa answered evasively, saying school was fine and he was making progress. Ahmed said he was being too modest and revealed that he'd won a math contest last spring. Tariq shrugged and asked when he'd last opened the Koran. When Moussa confessed he hadn't read it in awhile, Tariq said learning was a waste without it. He instructed his sons to attend mosque daily, warning them that a day would come when they would otherwise regret it. His words hardly came as a surprise. Soon after his arrest, he'd become more pious. Since then, he'd been scornful of Moussa's interests. And dismissed Ahmed's love of architecture as a waste of time.

"Two more minutes," the guard interjected.

"I want you to know," Tariq addressed the family, as they again tried to embrace him through the slit in the grill, "that at first I cursed the luck that landed me here. But with time to think, and friends to steer me, I now realize I was saved from a life of sin. I regret nothing. I am not unhappy. Don't think I'm trapped here like a dog in a kennel, but see me as a knife whose blade is being sharpened for a day of inevitable reckoning."

He then enjoined them not to stain the family's honour: a family without honour, he stressed, was like an olive grove without a source of water. He paused a moment and a change came over him. His features slackened, he started shaking, and he seemed to age before their very eyes. As a guard drew near, he started speaking in a rush, to the effect that he wished that all of them could stay, that he loved to hear their voices, and that he dreamed of being home and sleeping in his bed. He also yearned to be at the wedding, and cursed himself for being separate from his family.

The guard announced the visit was over. A second guard appeared and, opening a door at the back of the cell, escorted Tariq into a hallway. The old man just had time to yell, "Pray for me! Pray for me! And Moussa, be a man!"

And that was that. They were heading down a hallway to the crowded waiting room. From there they shuffled through the prison's east wing and made their way toward the building's exit, passing families who were still waiting for the privilege of spending fifteen minutes with their loved ones. And now they were hunting down a cab, which didn't come to the jail so often and were hard to flag down. But Moussa was oblivious. He wasn't thinking of the scalding heat, the hustle bustle, the long ride home, or the ache of seeing his *ab* confined. Instead he was dwelling on his father's words. "Be a man!" he had said. What did that mean? Exactly what had he been trying to say?

Come on, a voice whispered, *as if you don't know.*

CHAPTER SEVEN

The noise was indescribable. It sounded like an ogre clearing his throat. A moment later the volume grew so that it sounded more like a snorting bull, attacking from behind in a murderous fury. Then the noise was impossibly loud and hitting them from every side at once, as if a tsunami were pouring over the city. Avi flinched at the vibrations. And then he grinned.

Ten jets were flying in perfect formation. The first was metres ahead of three others, which were closely followed by another two, then a line of three and a lone one behind. All ten seemed to be inches from each other, and the trajectory of each was so beautifully timed that it was like watching one machine in motion, a mechanical Jewish star in motion.

The planes broke up and started to climb, releasing

streams of exhaust that were dyed blue and white. The crowd far below roared in approval, Avi as loud as anyone else.

It was *Yom Haatzmaut*, Israel's Independence Day. School had ended early, so he and two friends had walked to Zion Square, where they'd bought ice cream and were taking in the festivities. Musicians were scattered up and down Ben Yehuda Street: a brass trio was nearby; two violinists were playing a few metres down; and over in the distance a guy was strumming a banjo. There were even two pianists playing an upright piano that they'd hauled to the street with a mover's trolley. And, standing on a table in front of a café, was a man dressed up as David Ben Gurion, Israel's first head of state. In a stentorian voice he was reciting the speech that had marked the country's birth in 1948. His audience was applauding and waving flags ecstatically.

There were also lots of cops around: they were lining the street and standing two–three metres apart. On the nearby roofs more of them were visible, armed with rifles and tear-gas guns. Given the day's nature, and the high density crowds, there lurked the possibility of a bomb attack.

"Where is everybody?" Ilan asked.

"It isn't crowded enough?" Avi teased.

"He means the girls," Erez said. "They said they'd

meet us here. Ilan's holding his breath for Zohara."

"Zohara? That lefty! In your dreams!" Ilan sneered.

"I see the way you look at her. Pretty soon you're going to be handing out pamphlets. 'End the occupation! Hug a Palestinian!'"

"You're crazy! I'd never date a bleeding heart like her. Every time you wanted a kiss, she'd recite from Resolution 242. No thank you."

"If Prime Minister Rabin could shake hands with Chairman Arafat," Erez imitated the voice of a news broadcaster, "love can blossom between Zohara Stern and the right-wing extremist Ilan Safir."

"She reads too much," Ilan complained. "And her glasses make her look like an owl."

"If Sadat could shake hands with Menachem Begin, Ilan can get used to dating an owl." Erez could barely keep himself from laughing.

"And she's too sensitive," Ilan said. "I'll bet she's a vegetarian and wouldn't even eat *shwarma*. And she would make her boyfriend give up meat as well."

"If Israel could defeat its enemies in the Six Day War, Ilan can eat veggies to satisfy the peacenik Zohara." As he joked, Erez took a cigarette out.

"What are you doing?" Ilan asked.

"What does it look like I'm doing? I'm having a smoke."

"Are you crazy? You won't get into Golani if you're hooked on those. Hand them over!"

"Hey! Quit it! If I want to smoke, it's my personal business…!"

As his friends mock-wrestled, Avi studied the crowd. The musicians and actors were going full force, people were dancing, singing, and eating and, overall, the atmosphere was joyous. Then, he spied an old woman standing to one side. Her hair was white, she was very frail and her shoulders were draped with a worn, grey raincoat, despite the raging heat. She was also crying openly. Tears were streaming down her wrinkled cheeks. Avi was going to turn away in case she wanted privacy, but he was struck with the thought that she might require help.

"Excuse me," he spoke gently, "is everything okay?"

"Everything's fine, thank you," she replied, with a heavy foreign accent. She even laughed, only to start sobbing again.

"Are you sure?" he asked uncertainly.

"I get like this on *Yom Haatzmaut*," she said. "When I was your age and living in Poland, I never dreamed Jews would one day have an army and a place to call home. I can't tell you how beautiful this is. In Yiddish we would say *mechaia tsu sein a yid*. It's not so bad to be a Jew. But forgive a foolish senior and enjoy the day."

Smiling at the woman, Avi returned to his friends. Erez had a smoke in his mouth and Ilan was trying to yank it away. Still scuffling, Ilan yelled that they'd spotted Avi with his latest girlfriend and they'd never guessed that he liked older women.

The jets came screaming back overhead and Ilan and Erez stopped fooling around and watched as the F-18s laid claim to the sky. The crowd was spellbound. The planes were so fast, so unerring, so invincible that they seemed to promise the ants on the ground that no one would hurt them, no harm would ever come to pass, not when they were patrolling the heavens.

"The air force," Ilan sighed. "That's the place to be? How about it guys?"

"Count me in," Erez said.

"Me too," Avi seconded.

There was no point mentioning his fear of heights.

Moussa was heading down Al-Wad Road, was pushing a wheelbarrow laden with orders. He was fast approaching the Via Dolorosa. The street was almost empty, but for three vendors, an old Christian, and a group of boys, none of whom he recognized. There were five of them, no older than twelve. They were dragging a string of flags behind them — small, plastic Israeli flags. They must have grabbed them from the *yeshiva* down the road, home to Israeli religious students whose goal, it seemed, was to overrun the quarter with Jews. These boys were kicking the flags and spitting on them and treading them under foot.

One vendor smiled and cheered them on. The old Christian warned there were soldiers close by and the boys should take their fun elsewhere. They paid no attention.

One kid pulled out a box of matches. Striking a light, he set the flags on fire. The resultant smoke was heavy and black, and smelled toxic.

Moussa thought this was a bad idea, not only because it was a wild gesture but because it would draw the cops' attention. But what did he care? He had his work to look after.

"Excuse me. Coming through," he said.

The kids ignored him.

"Hey guys! I have a schedule to keep! Move aside."

"You want to join us? We have more flags to burn," the boy with the matches yelled. He was a sinewy, scabby, unscrubbed rat who looked like he'd thrown his share of stones at Israelis.

"I'm in a hurry. Some other time."

"You know what day it is?" The rat thought nothing of Moussa's size. He was standing not even a meter away, waving a flag in front of his face so that the smoke wafted into his lungs. "It's the worst day on the calendar, that's what it is. The least you can do is set a flag on fire."

"I have work to do."

"He has work," the rat cried out. "What do think we're doing?"

"I don't know. Fooling around?"

The rat-boy moved so quickly that he seemed to pull the knife from thin air. It had a six-inch blade with a serrated edge that looked like it had seen its share of use. Brandishing it expertly, he stabbed the air a few times.

"Still think I'm fooling around?"

It wasn't the knife that worried Moussa so much as the rat himself. His face was drawn in such a grimace of rage that his skin looked like it was ready to tear and expose the snarling skull below. Before Moussa could think of an appropriate answer, the flag's heavy flame reached the young brute's fingers, causing him to drop the plastic in pain. As he licked his hand, there was a raucous yell from further down. The smoke from the flags had attracted the police.

"Let's beat it," the rat screamed to his gang, flying down an alley with his knife in hand.

"Stop!" several policemen yelled, running after the kids at full tilt. The pedestrians on the scene didn't move aside but pretended to go about their daily business. One vendor had a cart full of apples, which he set at an angle to block the path and win the kids three extra seconds. A cop shoved the cart aside, toppling it over and sending the fruit everywhere. The vendor started yelling and demanding compensation, his curses tearing the air to shreds. His shouts triggered a volley of others. People had emerged from the nearby shops and faces were staring from a dozen windows, their mouths wide open, cursing the Jews. Several teens had sprouted from the earth and were volleying apples at the police.

The Israelis turned and faced their attackers, allowing the twelve-year old boys to returned and provoke them further. Apples were flying so thick and fast that the police took shelter in a nearby doorway and called for backup. They had pulled their guns out and might start shooting.

Moussa couldn't believe it. Two minutes ago the place had been peaceful and now it was hosting a miniature riot. It wasn't just that rat who was angry; the entire neighbourhood had exploded.

Pulling on his barrow, he retreated up the street. Plenty of apples lay nearby and no one would notice if he threw one at the police, but he wasn't even tempted. He wanted to go home.

As he pushed his way forward that, he considered that despite the three-year difference in age, that rat was twice the man he was.

CHAPTER EIGHT

Avi's team was on the field. Some were stretching and
limbering up, while a few were taking shots at the
goal. The heat was merciless. It felt more like August
than early May.

The team looked spiffy: each had sewn a blue
star on his shirt, to demonstrate their pride in *Eretz
Yisrael*. Yossi wasn't happy. He thought the symbol
would annoy the other team and alter the tone he was
hoping to achieve. Still, he let the issue pass. When
Chaim unfolded a flag, and planted it at their end of
the field, he told him to put the banner away. "Pride is
one thing," he'd stated. "Provocation another."

"So where are they?" Shimshon asked. "They're
twenty minutes late."

"They're scared," Erez said. "They know we're going to kick their butts."

"Unless they can't get organized. That's typical of them. They can never get their act together and that's why we beat them when we go to war." This said, Ilan hammered a ball past the goalie. "You'll have to do better than that!" he yelled at Yakovi.

Avi was about to charge a ball when Yossi gave a blast of his whistle. Their "guests" had finally arrived. They weren't alone: two Israeli cops were escorting them along. Avi's team moved in for a closer look.

Yossi and Rami embraced and shook hands. Before Rami could speak, a cop approached Yossi and asked if they were planning a game that day. When Yossi answered yes and motioned to his team, the cop turned to Rami and apologized curtly before walking away.

As the teams prepared themselves, Rami explained that, just outside the Damascus Gate, they'd drawn the notice of the cops on duty who'd been suspicious of the additions to their uniforms. In a fit of patriotism, he said with a chuckle, his players had sewn the national flag on their shirts, overruling his own objections. It was these flags that had drawn the cops' attention and caused them to scrutinize the group more closely. Yossi pointed to his team's Jewish stars. Both men shrugged and shared a good laugh.

"They have to beat us with their nationalism," Ilan grumbled.

"They have to rub their patriotism in our faces," Amir muttered.

"Let's get started!" the coaches called to their teams.

Avi watched the game unfolding in slow motion. Dribbling the ball misleadingly, he slid it past his opponent and pushed his way forward. Although he couldn't quite see Erez, instinct told him he was following behind, at something like a thirty degree angle. That was why, when two defenders closed in, he passed the ball and ... Erez received it. Running furiously, Avi plunged past the defensemen, one of whom was charging Erez, and feinted left then right again, to shake his own pursuer off. Meanwhile, Erez had kicked the ball to Chaim, who'd passed it to Erez who, with Avi open, sent it spinning in his direction. Because Avi was set at the wrong angle to receive it, he spun on his left foot, like a dancer pirouetting, stopped his turn and, in a rare and perfect arc of motion, kicked the ball with the side of his foot, his aim and timing beautifully in sync. He didn't even question whether the ball would reach its target: he knew it would.

His teammates cheered. He felt lighter than air.
The Palestinians were silent on their side of the field.

"It's like a geometry problem," Moussa was thinking. A man (A) is 8 metres off from teammate (B) and positioned at a 10 degree angle. A is being charged by 3 Israelis, 2 in front (I and II), the other (III) at a 30 degree angle. If A passes to B, I and II will hem B in, and the goalie (IV) will swing to his left. Boxed in, B will try to pass back to A, but III will intercept and ruin the play. Therefore A must pass to C who is 6 metres back and at a 260 degree angle. A must charge between I and II — who will close in on C — and veer 120 degrees. The ball will come from C and A will pass to B, who will be open as I and II will be distracted by A. IV will veer left, fearing a shot from B. As B receives the ball, A will swing 60 degrees. I and II will be 3 metres behind. IV will be to the left of A. B will pass, A will kick and … success will follow.

Moussa (A) passed to C (Amir), who quickly passed back to him. He then passed to Sami (B) who, divining his plan, returned the ball as IV moved left to cover the goal. Moussa kicked and … success did follow. His proof was done. QED.

His teammates cheered. He felt full of fire.

The Israelis were silent on their side of the field.

"It wasn't a foul!" Ilan raged. "Yossi shouldn't listen to that crap!"

"They don't deserve a kick!" Erez complained. "The Arab fell over his own big feet."

"I wasn't even close!" Chaim insisted. "There's no way I tripped him. And Yossi doesn't think so. You can tell by his expression."

Avi said nothing. He hadn't seen the error. The problem was the "foul" had occurred inside the box, and would give the Arabs a penalty kick. With two minutes left, and with the score 1–1, the Palestinians could win the game.

Moussa was standing off to one side. He was quiet and watching events in silence. As soon as he stopped running lethargy set in. He hadn't seen the so-called foul but Amir seemed so sure of himself.

"It's clear to a blind man," he kept insisting, "the ball was coming to me when that Jew tripped me up."

"I saw it. That's what happened," Sami agreed. "And Rami saw it too. As usual the Jews won't play by the rules."

"They've decided," Amir said.

"They've decided," Ilan yelled.

There was cheering when Rami said they were getting a free shot. "Stop cheering," he snapped. "They'll think we're gloating."

There were protests when Yossi announced the other team had won a free kick. "Stop groaning," he said. "They'll think we're poor sports."

As the Arabs encouraged their striker and the Israelis encouraged their goalie, Yossi and Rami threw their hands up in despair.

Amir eyed the goalie with the focus of a sniper. He was big and great at taking penalty shots. He was also confident that he could smash the ball in.

Yakovi watched Amir and the ball before him. He was small but wiry and lightning fast. He was confident that he could stop the ball.

Amir charged. He feinted left and Yakovi followed. The ball streaked forward, to Yakovi's right. He tried to twist mid-flight but was off by a hair.

The Palestinians cheered.

The Israelis were silent.

— • —

The Israelis were drinking sodas at the *makolet*. No one had spoken since they had left the field and the only sound audible was the occasional *psst* of a can being opened.

"I know what's in that hangar," Erez spoke, motioning to the building across the street from them.

"What?" Ilan said.

"It's where they hide dupes like Yossi who think we'll one day be at peace with the Arabs."

The Palestinians were on Al-Wad Road and enjoying a celebratory soda together. They were sitting and enjoying their triumph in silence and the only sound audible was the occasional *psst* of a can being opened.

"I know what's behind that doorway," Mahmoud spoke, motioning to the building across the lane from them.

"What?" Amir asked.

"It's where they stick idealists like Rami who think we'll one day be at peace with the Jews."

CHAPTER NINE

MAY 10, 2006 (WEDNESDAY): 3:45 P.M.

"We'll be ready in a moment. I want to check the equipment is working. Testing, testing, one two three."

Avi smiled. He was feeling nervous (what else was new). He was sitting in the living room with some juice in hand. Across from him, Phil Matthews was adjusting his recorder. A large man with large hands, a large head, and a large, warm smile, he was interviewing Avi at his dad's suggestion; he was a freelance journalist for the CBC and had been covering Israel for the last five years. He told Avi that he wasn't there to embarrass people or to champion one side over the over, but to capture people's sentiments on a range of issues. Avi could speak freely, he assured him, and if he didn't like his answers, they wouldn't be broadcast.

Shosh was suspicious. Even though Phil Matthews was her husband's friend, she distrusted journalists as a rule. "Reporters are like vultures," she liked to say. "They're always waiting for some corpse to feed on. Either they don't know our ways or they wilfully distort them to favour the Arabs."

"Alright, we're ready. Ignore the recorder. And don't tell me what you think I want to hear, but what you yourself sincerely believe. The best interviews are ones where people's honesty shines through. Okay?"

"I'll keep that in mind."

"Good. Let's get started. For the record, you're Avi Greenbaum, you live in West Jerusalem, and you moved to Israel in 2001."

"Yes."

"But your father's living in Toronto now?"

"He's a lawyer and couldn't leave his legal practice behind." There was more to it than that, he thought, but that's all Phil's listeners needed to know.

"I see. Okay, here's another easy question. What music do you listen to and what's your favourite movie?"

"I listen to jazz and classical mainly. I like some modern groups but my tastes are old-fashioned; my friends think I'm a freak that way. And my favourite movie is *Singing in the Rain*."

"Wow. Why *Singing in the Rain*?"

"It portrays a world that's only joyful. Don Lockwood and the others have nothing to fear. And the music could kill you, it's so perfect."

"Yeah, I can see that. So, tell me what it's like to live in West Jerusalem. It must be odd to have so much history around and to hear your city mentioned in the news so often?"

"Actually, it's no big deal. I do what everyone does — I go to school, listen to music, watch TV, and hang out with my friends. Sometimes I'll be walking around and the history jumps out, but that's more tiresome than anything else."

"Tiresome? Why? I would think it'd be interesting?"

"It would be if it came in small doses. As it is, it hits you wherever you go, good stuff sure, but bad stuff too. Take the old city. It has bullet-ridden walls from '48 and '67, and reminders of the Crusaders' siege, and signs of what the Romans did. Here in West Jerusalem, which is the modern part of town, there's the King David Hotel, which was blown up in the forties, and cafes and restaurants where attacks have taken place. So the city's special for its history, sure, but too often it tells you just how terrible things have been. Maybe that's why Canada's quiet: it was born just yesterday, compared to stuff over here."

"What about religion? It pervades the city. How does it affect you?"

"Well, when a siren goes off marking the start of *Shabbat*, everything slows and it's very peaceful."

"Do you go to synagogue?"

"No. This place is enough of a synagogue for me."

He was only partly joking. In that part of the world, the talk of God was exhausting. Avi felt sure that if God existed, He wouldn't think much of the hate He'd inspired, or of the bullying and violence committed in His name.

In March the family had gone for coffee at a local café. It was a Saturday, the one day all of them had off. No sooner had they installed themselves than three *Haredim* had wandered along and started shouting at them and hurling insults, saying they were breaking the Sabbath rules. When Dan had tried to calm them down, these "holy" guys practically spat at him. Much worse, of course, were the suicide bombers who, to express their devotion and commitment to God, maimed and killed in the name of Allah. It was possible that God had his place in the world — who was Avi Greenbaum to find fault with the Almighty — but people should be able to decide where God fit into their routines for themselves, instead of having holy rollers blast them with their narrow views. And if these guys were right and God approved of their actions? If God wanted them to bully people and force them on their knees and blow them to pieces? Then he wanted nothing to do with this God.

"Tell me this," Phil Matthews went on, "you arrived here only recently. I mean, you've been here, what, just under five years. Do you feel like you belong?"

"Sure. Most people here are from somewhere else. As a Canadian Jew, I don't stick out." But he sure did, as a fearful Jew.

"And the Palestinians? Where do they fit in?"

"I'm not sure I understand your question."

"Well, do you have any Palestinian friends?"

"No."

"Do you have Arab classmates?"

"No. There isn't a single Arab at my school."

"And your neighbours?"

"Most are Jewish, with some Christians mixed in."

"So where do you meet Palestinians?"

"I see them around, I guess, because we're near the Old City. And lots of them have jobs in our part of town. And we see them in the Muslim Quarter, but even ..." he broke off with a shrug.

"But you're playing soccer against an Arab team?"

"Yeah. But once we've played, we go back home."

"So they're strangers?"

"Yes."

"You don't find this odd?"

"I don't know. It's normal here, for Jews and Muslims."

In actual fact he did find it odd. When touring the Muslim *shuk* one time — when his family had just moved to the Musrara region — he'd been struck by how different the Arabs were, with their language, their dress, their houses, their religion. Even their choice of car was different: they drove Peugeots, not Subarus like most Israelis.

He had asked his mother about this divide. Her response had been matter-of-fact: "How often do ethnic groups in Canada mix? I grew up in Toronto and never brought a Tamil home. How often did I talk to Natives? How many Jamaicans or Sikhs did I know? I greeted the Koreans living on our street, sure, but they had their friends and we had ours." While the gulf between Jew and Arab was extreme, she agreed, the fact was most ethnic groups stuck to themselves. In other words, Israelis were just like other populations. It seemed to make sense, but Avi still had his doubts.

"How do you feel," Matthews continued, "when you hear Palestinians can't live in Israel, the ones who were expelled in '48 at least? Isn't it strange when you consider they've been here for generations?"

"You mean the Palestinians in refugee camps?"

"Among others."

"I feel bad for them."

"But shouldn't they be Israeli? You're a citizen after all. You arrived here only recently, and yet you enjoy many rights these people can't have. Isn't that ironic?"

"I guess. But Israel's a Jewish state. The right to settle here is mine by birth. This policy guarantees that the state stays Jewish, even though it does leave the refugees out in the cold."

"It doesn't trouble you that the state is Jewish?"

"Why should it? I'm happy there's a state for Jews."

Avi felt like yawning. It wasn't that these questions bored him, or that he thought them unimportant. It was just the frequency with which these discussions took place and how, for all the talk, there was never a concrete conclusion. How many times had Rachel and his mom debated? Had either of them budged? Not even an inch. And the TV showed egg heads butting skulls together, one arguing for the Arabs, the other against. Was there ever any progress? Not on your life. And the same was true of the foreign press and university professors and politicians. No one was willing to abandon his opinion. So what was the point? Why expel this hot air? Why didn't people simply throw up their hands and accept that Jews and Arabs would fight forever? It would make life easier for all parties involved and wouldn't give rise to any false hopes.

"Tell me about Canada," Phil Matthews said, sensing he had gone far enough with this subject. "What do you miss?"

"My family and I discussed this subject recently. I miss certain foods, snow, Saturday night hockey, and family road trips."

"You don't take road trips here?"

"We do sometimes. But when we travel north, we hit the Lebanese border. And if we drive to the Golan, we approach Syria and Jordan. The south is no better. Once you've reached Eilat, you're faced with Jordan and Egypt."

"You're really boxed in, eh? What else do you miss?"

"I miss the freedom from politics. Here, politics is everything. Our soccer match? That's politics. When you go into a store or bank, a guard will search you. Politics. The garbage bins on public streets? They're reinforced to take an explosion — politics again. On my birthday, what did we discuss at supper? Politics, politics, and more politics. I'm not just a kid who likes jazz and soccer; in the eyes of the world I'll be a soldier in three years and come to oppress my share of Arabs. I hate it. I mean, Israel's cool, but the constant show of politics can wear you down."

"Why do you think people are so interested in Israel?"

"I've wondered that too. It's politics again, I think. Most Westerners have boring lives, politically speaking — Canada for example. They like to watch our politics play out, the way they'll cheer at a hockey fight on TV. But they can turn the TV off; we have to live in this political swamp."

"You have a point," Phil Matthews confessed. "Here's one last question. Are there advantages to living in a place like Israel?"

"Advantages? How do you mean?"

"Do you get something here that you can't find anywhere in Canada, say?"

Avi considered the question. It was exactly the one his father had asked when he'd started to doubt their *aliyah*: "Why are we here? What do we gain? And don't mention all that Jewish stuff because we can be Jewish in Canada too." And even if there was a gain, it came at a price. It required you to shelve your fears and to do what men are supposed to do. Still, he couldn't say as much on public radio, and that's why he went with his mother's response.

"Maybe our lives are richer," he said. "We have to fight for any peace we enjoy — I know that sounds crazy, to fight for peace. Still, because we have to fight for it, maybe we treasure it more. And my mom says she's never met a boring Israeli: it's the reward we get from being on edge all the time."

After thanking him and saying he'd like to visit again, Phil Matthews put the recorder away, stood, and stretched his limbs. Shosh, who'd been sitting in the kitchen all this while, came into the room and said she thought it'd gone well. The journalist agreed and said he wasn't just being polite: he would like to return in a couple of weeks. He mentioned several dates in June, then shook their hands, and left.

From the balcony Avi watched him walking away. For a moment he wanted to call him back and have him erase every word he'd recorded. But, just as suddenly he didn't care: there were so many words in circulation already, a lot of them more stupid than anything he'd come out with, that his version of events couldn't do any harm. And if he got people debating again, well, it was to be expected.

CHAPTER TEN

We were pulled from you half-grown
Our mother Palestine
And heard your anguished cries from afar
As foreign hands defiled you
And strange lands raised us to manhood
Indifferently, because we were not
The issue of their womb.
We see you shed tears of stone
And, in deference to your sorrow,

Rain these tears upon your aggressors.

Once the reader had finished reciting this poem, a song started playing over the school's PA system. The lyrics came from Fadwa Tuqan's poem "The Call of the

Land." It was the tale of a refugee's return to Palestine, even though he knows he will die in the process.

As the song continued, and his fellow students listened raptly, Moussa couldn't stop worrying about his *jadda*. She was always nervous and prone to sadness, but especially so on *Nakba* Day. Who could blame her? With all the talk about 1948 and the expulsion of the people from their ancestral lands, how couldn't she brood on her personal pain?

He tried to imagine her as a twelve-year-old girl — he peeled away her wrinkles and fragile limbs and pictured her running through the family's olive grove. And on that day, April 9, 1948? He'd read accounts of the attack on Deir Yassin, but these were nothing compared to her description, which she always recited in a thin, dry voice, as if she'd shed so many tears as a child that the source for fresh ones had run permanently dry.

It was early morning and she was awoken by the sound of shots and people clamouring wildly. For weeks the villagers had hoped to avoid the war that had broken out when Israel's birth had been announced. But now the beast was at their doorstep. *Jadda*'s father and two brothers left to join the defenders. The battle waged on. The gunfire intensified, with the added sound of exploding grenades. Her mother couldn't make up her mind: should she flee with her daughters or wait for the men to return? Finally, after an eternity of waiting, the firing stopped. But that was when the nightmare started.

In halting Arabic they were told to leave their houses. When people hesitated, a rough voice announced that their men were dead or had fled the village and left them to their fate. Surrender was their only option. Muttering a prayer, her *um* had led her daughters outside. As his *jadda* went to follow, her sleeve caught on a nail by the door and she stopped to work the material free. Suddenly, she heard her mother's screams followed immediately by machine-gun fire so close to the house it would leave her deaf in one ear. She watched her oldest sister fall. When recounting the tale, she would pause at this point and ask her audience the very same question: if it takes so long to fashion a human, how can everything so terribly precious, all the love and dedication invested, vanish in less time it takes a child to swallow?

She hid beneath a bed for hours. When the enemy discovered her, they led her past her family's bodies — her middle sister Eman had died while clutching her *um*. Some men loaded her onto a truck with other children. She remembers driving out of the village and seeing bodies strewn all over: her father and brothers were among the dead. She remembers the long drive into Jerusalem. She remembers the wails of the children beside her who had also witnessed the deaths of their loved ones — 110 people she would later learn. She remembers being forced from the truck at the entrance to the Jaffa Gate, which she'd visited before with her parents beside her. On that occasion her *ab* had treated her to ice cream. There was no ice cream that day in April.

"But there are good people too," she would always conclude. A woman eventually stumbled on the children — Hind Husseini, of blessed memory — and cared for them and housed them in an orphanage. But the damage had been done of course: her family, her house, her land, her history, her future, her happiness, all had been taken. The thieves had robbed her of everything. Everything.

When he was little, Moussa had told his mother that he wanted to make his *jadda* smile. His mother had answered, "Good luck to you. I have tried all my life and never succeeded. She will smile when the past no longer insults her."

Clearly that day was a long ways off.

He had the idea to buy his *jadda* chocolate on his way home from school, so she could pass the day with a sweet taste in her mouth.

— • —

"What do you see?" Their teacher was standing in front of a map of Israel. It was covered in Hebrew and showed no Arabic whatever.

"What do you see?" he asked again, this time with impatience.

"It is a map," Mahmoud said, "of the land the Zionists stole."

"That is correct," Ali said with approval. "But let us investigate this statement in greater detail. For the sake of simplicity, let's concentrate on al-Quds — Jerusalem as the Zionists call it. Over here, for example, we have an area called Malcha."

"That's over by the mall," Sami said. "I was there last month."

"It is a fine complex," Ali agreed. "I too have visited it on many occasions. But while I wandered its stairs and halls and stores, I was treading on the ruins of the village al-Mahila."

The students were shocked. They had explored the mall, too, but hadn't guessed it lay on top of Arab ruins.

"I never liked the place," Mahmoud said. "Now I know why."

"On our map, or rather, their map," Ali continued, "we see the name Mevasseret Zion, which is home to the world's first kosher McDonald's. But long before Jews ate their hamburgers here, Palestinians were living in the village of Qalunya."

"I will never eat a hamburger again," Anwar declared.

"Here is Moshav Naham — it was once the Arab town Artuf. Here is Nes Harim, which used to be Dayr al-Shaykh. Ramat Raziel was our village Kasla, Mevo Beitar was our village al-Qabu, and the Kfar Shaul Mental Health Centre has been built on remnants of Deir Yassin."

Moussa started at this mention of his *jadda*'s former village.

"And al-Burayj, Bayth Mahisr, Allar, Satuf, Jashar, Islin, the list goes on, all of these are gone. What were villages or thriving towns have vanished altogether, existing only as memories for the families who lost them. And this is just the Jerusalem area. To do justice to our *Nakba*, we would have to discuss 400 villages and 700,000 people who were dispossessed of everything."

Population is based on exponential growth, Moussa thought. If every family produced four children, these 700,000 souls (assuming they formed 350,000 couples) would have produced 1,400,000 descendants. And if their children had followed their example, they would have yielded 2,800,000 Palestinians. And they would have yielded millions in turn. But all of them were living abroad — in Jordan, Syria, Lebanon, Tunis, the United States, Canada, in every place imaginable except their native soil. His brother Douad could be counted among them.

"Sometimes I wonder," Ali reflected, standing by the window and watching a crowd parade outside, "how it is our *shebab* can confront the Jewish army. I wonder how our mothers can stand to sacrifice their children. I ask myself, especially, how our people can strap bombs to their chests and blow themselves and some Zionists to pieces. The explanation lies on the map before you. Once you grasp its implications, you will understand the anger that pushes us to act. If you learn only one thing from the time we have spent together, let it be this map and the sorrow it embodies."

The class was silent. His friends were frowning, and Moussa was staring hard at the map. It didn't strike him as a piece of paper; it seemed more like the lid on an unbreakable coffin.

Yet still he felt as hollow as an abandoned tomb.

"I'm saying we have lots to atone for, that's all."

Zohara sipped her coffee. She and Avi were in a café down on Hillel Street. They had finished rehearsing early that day and decided to go out for coffee at last. Whereas Avi had wanted to discuss their trip to England, Zohara had been focusing on *Nakba* Day. As they strolled together, she had rambled on about the expulsion of Arabs and the stolen houses and Deir Yassin. When they'd reached the café and ordered coffee, Avi had proposed they split a piece of pastry. No, she'd snapped. She was avoiding sweets to mark the day. And while drinking her coffee — black of course — she'd kept saying how disastrous the war in '48 had proven.

"It would have been better had we lost," she said, sipping her coffee. She grimaced at its bitter taste.

Avi eyed her closely. Despite the gruelling temperature outside, she looked cool as ice cream and self-possessed. She was wearing a green shirt that was freshly pressed and tucked into a graceful cotton skirt. She wore no makeup, no jewellery, and no adornments, with the exception of her sunglasses whose lenses were a bright shade of yellow. Her eyes were sensitive to the light, she explained, and without such lenses she couldn't go outside.

"That war marked our original sin and from it all our crimes have emerged."

Avi sighed. He wasn't in the mood for politics. On the other hand, he felt she had gone too far and he didn't want her inferring from his silence that he in any way agreed with her.

"What about the invasion?" he asked. "It isn't worthwhile mentioning?"

"The invasion?"

"You know what I mean. You think it's nothing that, after the partition plan, five armies gathered with a view to destroy us — in violation of international opinion? What would have happened if the Arabs had defeated us? Do you think they would have shared the land or drowned us in the sea?"

"You're arguing that survival always comes first. I'm saying it doesn't, not at the expense of a Deir Yassin."

"It was terrible, I agree. But it's not like anyone says otherwise. Our government even apologized at the time and promised such a massacre wouldn't happen again."

"And that's why they expelled over half the country's Arabs?"

Again Avi sighed. He knew this history well. Their teacher, Shulamit, had covered this subject in detail and never once substituted myths for facts. She had exposed the class to accounts from both sides, they had combed through statistics and watched several films, including one about Deir Yassin. And several veterans had addressed the class, talking about how proud they'd been to fight in the campaign, while acknowledging the hardships of war. One seasoned old man had started to cry when he'd recalled the death of his younger brother: he'd promised his mother he would protect him from harm. "Why did they have to attack us?" he'd lamented.

In other words, Avi could easily have argued with Zohara. He could have said, for example, that there were Palestinians who'd helped the invading forces, while others had freely vacated their homes so the Arab armies could target Jews directly without worrying that their fellow Arabs would get caught in the fire. All right, it was questionable that the Jews had expelled lots of innocent Arabs, ones who'd been careful to steer clear of the conflict, but the times had been desperate: it had only been three years since the Nazi nightmare had ended, and the Jews had felt, with ample reason, that they could either fight or face liquidation.

They had done what men must do.

But he kept his mouth shut: he'd learned from watching his family debate that there was no hope of changing people's opinions. He and Zohara could argue for hours, but she would still feel that the Jews had been wrong, and he would still think she was overreacting.

He was silent for a second reason. The café was a spacious room. It was fairly crowded for that time of day and, among the customers, was a strange-looking man. He was sitting by himself in a corner, and wasn't drinking coffee or eating any pastry. He was dark-complexioned and had neutral features; he might have been Jewish, he might have been Muslim. An over-sized briefcase lay at his feet, and he was dressed in a coat that was buttoned to his neck. Every ten seconds he checked his watch.

"You're not listening," Zohara said with a smile. "Does that mean you're not interested or are you signaling defeat?"

"Look at that guy. Does he seem a little nervous? No, don't stare at him."

"The one in the corner? He looks normal enough…. No, he does seem nervous. And he could be Jewish or…."

"He's lifting his briefcase."

"It seems heavy by the looks of it. What's inside?"

"He's sweating too. And his jacket's fully buttoned. I don't like this."

"I don't either. He really is creepy. Should we tell the waiter…?"

"It's *Nakba* Day. You know what that means?"

"He's out to make some gesture maybe. They warned as much on the radio. Look — he consulted his watch again."

"We should phone someone.... Or maybe we should leave."

Avi was sweating and Zohara no longer look so cool. Should they throw some money on the table and go? But what about the others? They might pay a price. They could phone someone, but that might draw his attention. Unless Avi suddenly rushed the creep. If he were quick enough, he could knock him out or maybe pin his arms. But the guy was big and could fend him off. And, besides, it wouldn't work. He could feel his fear eroding his muscles, wearing away at the Israeli within.

"He's reaching in his pocket." Zohara could barely breath. "He's got his cellphone out. But ... he's holding it."

"Maybe it's a detonator."

"Okay. Look. Let's just leave. I'll put fifty shekels down and we'll both walk out. Are you ready?"

"I'm not sure...."

"I want to go. On the count of three...."

She dropped a fifty shekel note on the table and climbed to her feet. When Avi remained seated, she grabbed him by the shoulder and yanked him upwards. The two of them made their way to the exit. With every step, Avi dreaded the worst, certain he would hear a click, a thunderous roar, then nothing at all. As they were crossing the threshold, someone else stepped inside, a twenty-year-old man with shocking red hair. Avi thought he should warn this person, but the guy was in too much of a hurry.

Once outside Avi wanted to run. He wanted to get far away from the place and track a policeman down, someone who could do what real men do. But he didn't know the name of the place. As his eyes searched the store for a sign, he got a look inside. The redhead was sitting with the creepy guy and gesturing in a way that suggested he was sorry. Avi and Zohara paused. The suspected bomber had lifted the bag and was placing it with the cellphone in the young man's lap. The bag was open and packed with books. The top ones were covered in Hebrew writing.

Zohara was looking at the waiter now. He had approached their table and pocketed her money. He was smiling in triumph and who could blame him? She had overpaid by forty shekels.

Avi looked at her and was just about to make a joke. It really was funny how they'd overreacted, never mind the guy had fit the terrorist's profile. But Zohara was angry and walking away. It could have been the fact that she'd wasted so much money, but Avi suspected it was something else: she resented the ease with which her suspicions had been triggered, despite her "universal" point of view. Or she'd sensed something in Avi that had turned her off; or, rather, she had failed to detect the right sort of stuff.

Either way, it was too bad. He'd just been getting used to her smile.

CHAPTER ELEVEN

Olympic Airways flight 512, destination Athens, Greece, is beginning to board at gate 54. Passengers are asked to have their documents ready.

Hearing this departure announcement, Moussa felt his spirits soar. Was there anything as exciting as a major airport? If he went upstairs to the departure hall, he would enter a corridor with multiple gates and each could take him halfway across the world, to New York, Athens, Cairo, Tokyo, Singapore, Ottawa, London, Paris, places where you weren't expected to be angry and men could spend their days studying mathematics. Life here was just one possibility among thousands.

This is the final call for Lufthansa Flight 105 for Frankfurt, Germany. Passengers are requested to board at gate 32 and to have their documents ready for inspection.

"Is there anything more exciting than an airport?" Ahmed asked.

Moussa had to laugh: he wasn't the only one who felt this way! Together he and Ahmed studied the airport with ill-concealed looks of admiration. They were standing in a spacious hall whose walls and arches were made of Jerusalem stone and whose tiled floors were blindingly bright. In the lobby's center was an imposing skylight that housed an ingenious fountain: the water seemed to fall from out of nowhere. And scattered around the enormous space were benches, tables, and padded armchairs, along with plants and other decorations. Electronic panels screened the arrival and departure times: there were dozens of flights coming and going. It was a lovely space, large enough to hold vast crowds, yet comfortable and charming to stroll in.

"What I like best about airports," Ahmed observed, "is not just the planes taking off, but people's frame of mind. Everyone is at his best in such a building. They are either leaving home and excited to be flying; or they're returning from some place and can't wait to see their family."

As if to illustrate this point, a man emerged from a doorway, pushing a cart that was crammed with baggage. He looked tired and unshaven and a little confused; but his face glowed when he spied a boy run towards him, ahead of a woman and other children. The man looked like he was ready to explode with joy.

United Airways Flight 517 to Washington is now boarding at Gate 37A. Passengers are requested to have all documents in hand.

"Will Douad be happy to be back, you think?" Moussa asked. "On the phone he said Canada was the Garden of Eden."

"Weddings are always happy occasions. And while Douad is happy in Canada, he knows his place is here."

"I'm not so sure he would agree with you."

"We'll find out soon," Ahmed observed, motioning to the arrivals screen. Flight AC 846, Douad's flight number, was flashing. The plane had landed safely.

"We just have time to buy some candies," Ahmed continued. "They'll guarantee his visit goes sweetly."

"Dad's flight has arrived. I can't believe it's on time."

Avi followed Rachel's pointing finger and, sure enough, the arrival screen showed that flight AC 846 had landed safely. He felt a rush of excitement. Soon his dad would emerge from a doorway, an oddly familiar and comforting sight even if he hadn't seen him in ages. As always happened when he thought about his

father, a hundred images came to mind: his dad singing as he piloted the car, dealing cards in a tent while
camping, skating with the family at Nathan Phillips
Square, napping on a couch, and cutting the lawn.
There were less pleasant pictures, too, of him wanting
to leave Israel, packing his bags, and disappearing.

"When was he last here?" Rachel asked.

"He came last September, for Rosh Hashanah."

"That's right. I don't like that we see so little of him."

"You don't think he'll try to live here again? Like,
in ten years maybe, when he's ready to retire?"

"Dan would say yes. He still thinks dad went back
so he could pay our bills and that his heart is really
with us. But it isn't that simple."

"No. Probably not."

"Israel isn't for everyone. Dad has his strengths,
but he's missing what it takes to survive over here."

"What does it take to survive?" As if he didn't know.

"A number of things," she replied. "But I clued
into the important one soon after we arrived. Do you
remember that dog?"

"How could I forget?" Avi was blushing. They
had been living in a well-heeled neighbourhood, in
a six-story building with a spacious courtyard. He'd
been playing in this courtyard by himself one morning when a large German shepherd appeared without

warning. The dog growled and bared its teeth. He had tried to escape to the building's entrance, but the dog blocked him and continued barking. He yelled for his parents because their unit faced the courtyard, and his dad had heard him and rushed downstairs. He not only confronted the dog but, discovering it belonged to the building's landlord, asked the guy angrily how he could leave this drooling brute unleashed.

"I heard dad yell at the landlord," she went on. "But the guy didn't apologize or even bat an eyelid. Instead he said the sooner you faced your fears, the sooner you'd fit into the country's fabric. 'We can't be afraid in Israel,' he said. And the more I think about it, the more I agree. And dad agreed too. That's why he decided to leave."

Avi nodded. He had nothing to say. Once again, he was hearing that men had to step up; either that or they should think about moving elsewhere. As his sister continued to scan for their father, he glanced up at the electronic screens. There were planes departing for Athens, Paris, London, Rome, New York City, Rio de Janeiro. He could always leave, if he so saw fit. If he couldn't meet the general standard, there were other places where he could blend in well.

He'd keep it in mind. Although the prospect of running off was hardly reassuring.

— • —

"Was he on board?"

"Of course. He would have called otherwise."

"But it's been an hour since the plane touched down."

Moussa could see that his brother was anxious. He was no longer pointing out the airport's features and explaining how the skylight and fountain fit beautifully together. He was imagining the worst. He was thinking Douad had been stopped by the authorities and was seated in a backroom and being asked all sorts of questions. "Are you the son of Tariq Shakir? Who's your boss in Hamas? Who're you working for in Islamic Jihad?" The announcements and screen updates, far from stirring his excitement, had him on the verge of screaming in frustration.

"Where is he?" he asked again. "Everyone is gone. The cops must be holding him in detention."

"They're waiting too," Moussa said, pointing to two people further down the hall, a brother and sister by the looks of it. The male looked familiar somehow.

"It's a good thing I have the name of our lawyer. But it'll do no good if they've tossed him in jail, the sons of bitches."

"It's been only half an hour."

"It takes a minute to arrest a man and change his life forever! Maybe I should speak to someone."

"He'll come out. You'll see."

"You have to shake a tree to get the fruit! You were born in this country and you still don't know that…?"

"There. What did I tell you?"

Moussa pointed down the hallway where a door had opened and a man had emerged.

"*Alhamdulilah*," Ahmed said, his voice cracking with relief. "Douad! Over here!"

Spotting them, the figure ran forward, a smile splitting his face in two. Ahmed ran to him, followed by Moussa. It was strange. He'd expected Douad to look older but, if anything, he seemed younger and much less careworn. All three brothers embraced simultaneously.

"You call that luggage? One small suitcase?"

"I'm not here long. And I assumed if I traveled lightly, the customs guards would speed me along. But they were more suspicious than ever. You wouldn't believe how closely they checked my papers and how carefully they searched every hollow in my suitcase. I see nothing's changed…. Hey!"

He laughed as Ahmed showered Douad with candies. Some people in the vicinity applauded. When the candies stopped flowing, the brothers hugged again.

"Come on," Ahmed urged, retrieving the candies from the floor. "We have a long ride back. The next bus leaves in fifteen minutes. You can tell us everything as soon as we're seated."

"There's nothing to tell," Douad said. "Except that Canada's the Promised Land."

The trio headed to the airport's exit, laughing and swapping the latest news. As they neared the door that led to the bus ramps, they passed a group of soldiers who were drinking cans of soda. They were carrying M-16s and sported red berets: Golani. For an instant Douad fell deathly silent, surprised by the familiar sight he hadn't seen in ages. But he caught himself and started joking again.

As everyone waited for the bus to arrive, he was careful to keep his bag between himself and the soldiers.

"Where is he?" Avi moaned, "It's taking forever."

"He'll be out soon. He fell into the clutches of a bureaucrat, that's all."

"Those other people met their guy," Avi said, motioning to Moussa and his brothers at a distance. He thought he'd met the younger one once but was too distracted to figure out where. "So what on earth is keeping him?"

"He's using his Canadian passport, I'll bet. He always hated his Israeli one. He said it was like wearing a target on your heart. Knowing him, he's thrown it away. Anything to keep strangers from suspecting he might be an Israeli, God forbid."

"Can they penalize him for that? Or keep him overnight? Maybe we should say something…?"

"There he is!" his sister cried. "*Abba!* Over here!"

Avi glanced to his right and … his dad was visible. He was hauling a suitcase on wheels behind him and was clutching onto a mass of papers. His eyes were ringed and he had a five o'clock shadow, but he was smiling widely and was a welcome sight. And despite his fatigue, he looked healthy, happy and free of worries. Avi felt his spirits soar. As always happened when his dad appeared, he appreciated just how much he'd missed him. Like Rachel, he was racing forward. Seconds later, all three Greenbaums were embracing.

"I'm sorry it took so long. They went through my documents with a fine-toothed comb."

"You used your Canadian passport," Rachel said accusingly.

"That's right. I couldn't find my Israeli one. It

took a while to sort things out but it's no big deal. You both look well."

"We can talk as we drive," Rachel said. "If we don't leave now, the traffic will be terrible."

Avi took his father's bag. As the three of them strode towards the parking lot entrance, his father started asking questions: how was school, was she getting cold feet, was their mother okay, had Avi met Phil Matthews?

When they walked by the exit for the buses, where the Golani soldiers were milling about, a shadow crossed Mr. Greenbaum's features; just as suddenly he smiled and resumed the conversation.

It had never been so clear before: when one factored out his family, he had no business being there.

CHAPTER TWELVE

MAY 20, 2006 (SATURDAY): 2:30 P.M.

"We'll be ready in a moment. I'm just testing this equipment. Hello, hello, one two three."

Moussa suppressed his nervousness. Why was he nervous? He was seated in the living room, his mother was nearby, and Douad was sitting upstairs on the roof, smoking no doubt and throwing crumbs to some pigeons. And Phil Matthews seemed unusually kind, as did the interpreter accompanying him, a scrawny guy from a West Bank village with a crazy accent.

It was the idea of being recorded that he didn't like. When he spoke into the recorder, his voice would be broken into digitalized signals, which would be carried as a WAV file to a studio in Canada and played across the country, from one coast to the other. Would he, Moussa Shakir, be heard in the mountains, or the forests with the grizzly bears, or an Eskimo igloo? They had Eskimos in Canada, right? How strange that people lived in structures of snow. Unless these stories were exaggerations, as happens when people discuss cultures that are strange to them. The Eskimos maybe thought he slept in a tent and traveled by camel and ate nothing but dates, whereas his favourite food was hamburgers and French fries.

"Alright, let's start," Phil Matthews said. "For the record, you are Moussa Shakir and you live on Al-Wad Road in East Jerusalem. Your family has lived here for many generations and owns a store in the nearby *shuk*."

"That's correct," Moussa said, once the *Daffawiyya* had translated these words, most of which he'd understood already.

"Okay. Tell us Moussa. Do you have any hobbies and what's your favourite movie?"

"I like studying mathematics. And my favourite movie is *The Lord of the Rings*. The last segment in the trilogy is the best, in my opinion. And I love playing soccer."

"You play against an Israeli team, don't you?"

"Yes. We have played each other twice. Soccer is

something we share in common. And just wait until the World Cup starts. We'll be glued to the TV."

"We do the same in Canada with our hockey playoffs."

While Moussa liked Phil Matthews, he was different from the people knew. He looked like he didn't have a care in the world. He seemed like someone who was used to his freedom, who could roam the world without fearing the police, who assumed that when he smiled at someone, he would be smiled at in return. While attractive, such behaviour was childish, naive. In fact, Moussa doubted strongly this man could grasp the situation here: he could sympathize with one side or the other, but he could never understand the stakes involved or come up with a workable solution. He couldn't feel anger so what did he know?

But Moussa wasn't angry either so who was he to fault this man?

The *Daffawiyya* was a different matter. The lines on his face and the bags around his eyes revealed that this place was no mystery to him. He also wore a look of envy. He envied Moussa his place in Jerusalem. He envied him his Israeli status and access to services like everyone else and his ID card that allowed him to roam about freely and his removal from the West Bank's hardships, with Israeli troops always interfering.

"If you think you have it rough," his look suggested, "you have no idea how lucky you are."

The interpreter was angry. He could do what men were expected to do, easily.

"… Let's get back to your taste in movies," Phil Matthews said, "*Lord of the Rings* is an interesting choice. Can you tell me why you like it so much?"

"Because it describes a situation that is black and white. And good ends up defeating evil."

"I see. Do you feel it symbolizes your struggle here?"

"Sometimes. I often think the eye of Sauron is watching."

"We should note, for our radio audience, that your father is in prison right now."

"That's correct."

"And he was arrested because he was helping terrorists?"

"He imports produce from all over the West Bank. Explosives were found in a sack of flour."

"Was he aware of them?"

"No. Well, it's hard to say. Some say yes — the Israeli police for example. Others say no — my mother and my relatives. And some say he had no choice in the matter. If he'd refused to smuggle these explosives in, some dangerous people would have been very angry."

"If you think you have it rough," his look suggested, "you have no idea how lucky you are."

The interpreter was angry. He could do what men were expected to do, easily.

"… Let's get back to your taste in movies," Phil Matthews said, "*Lord of the Rings* is an interesting choice. Can you tell me why you like it so much?"

"Because it describes a situation that is black and white. And good ends up defeating evil."

"I see. Do you feel it symbolizes your struggle here?"

"Sometimes. I often think the eye of Sauron is watching."

"We should note, for our radio audience, that your father is in prison right now."

"That's correct."

"And he was arrested because he was helping terrorists?"

"He imports produce from all over the West Bank. Explosives were found in a sack of flour."

"Was he aware of them?"

"No. Well, it's hard to say. Some say yes — the Israeli police for example. Others say no — my mother and my relatives. And some say he had no choice in the matter. If he'd refused to smuggle these explosives in, some dangerous people would have been very angry."

"I see. I must say you sound very calm. Still… when the Israelis jailed your father, would say they were protecting themselves?"

"I understand they need protection. But we have needs too. We need our freedom badly, for example."

"How aren't you free? I mean, when you compare yourself to an Israeli teen — I interviewed a teen last week — what is he permitted that you can't have?"

Moussa considered Matthews closely. This question of freedom was a difficult topic and wasn't just a matter of Arab versus Jew. From the TV shows and movies he'd watched, he thought Westerners were free in a way he didn't agree with. It was one thing to be free to control your own land, to follow your customs, or to travel without roadblocks; it was quite another to act solely for yourself, to ignore the constraints of tradition and family, and for men and women to mix freely together.

When he saw TV shows about men getting drunk, or cursing foully, or parading tattoos, he always wondered how these people could behave so badly. Why weren't they arrested by the police or, at least, upbraided by their family? But family for such people was a problem, too. These hoodlums never had parents or siblings, or if they did, they lived in a separate world, and never sent home money or phoned to say hi or expressed their respect for the parents who'd raised them.

But the greatest puzzle was their treatment of women. Moussa knew a few Arab women who had gone to university, but none would ever wander on her own or live by herself or have boyfriends.... Boyfriends! For a woman to behave like the rock star Madonna, to bare her face and legs and mid-riff, was disgusting, crazy, and shameful. How could her father or brothers allow it? Did these western-ers have no sense of *irdh*? Was this the freedom Phil Matthews intended, the freedom to behave like ani-mals and madmen?

But then again who was he to speak? He couldn't do what men must do and his notion of *irdh* was artificial.

"He can travel without showing his papers," he answered instead. "He never gets delayed at check-points. He can live where he wants, do what he wants, and work at any job he's been trained to perform. His children will be citizens and the state will support him. These are freedoms I cannot take for granted."

"How well do you know Israelis? Do you have any Jewish friends, for example?"

"None." Moussa almost laughed. The idea of a Jewish friend struck him as absurd.

"There aren't any Jews in your school?"

"Why would Jews attend my school? We are all Palestinian. Let the Jews attend their schools and let us stick to ours."

"When you hear the word 'Jew,' how do you feel?"

"I feel … surprised. They are fearful that we are plotting against them."

"Are you plotting against them?"

"Me?" He laughed, secretly pleased. Perhaps Phil Matthews saw some element that made him uneasy. "No. I'm not plotting."

"But some people are."

"You mean the suicide bombers?"

"Yes."

"They are very angry. But such anger is destructive."

"So you disapprove of them?"

"Yes, I disapprove." That was true but he envied them too. To feel such anger! All one's doubts would disappear!

"Okay. But tell me. If you could speak to Prime Minister Olmert, what advice would you give? What could he do to bring about peace?"

"That's simple. I would tell him to stop meddling and to return our land, starting with my *jadda*'s farm in Deir Yassin."

"Your grandmother is from Deir Yassin?"

"Yes. She lived through the massacre. She was twelve years old."

"Do you think the Prime Minister would follow your advice?"

"Why should the strong give in to the weak?"

"So what's the solution?

Moussa shook his head. Had Phil Matthews never heard of incompleteness, Kurt Gödel's theory in mathematics? It said there are true statements about the natural numbers that can't be proven using the rules of the system. Similarly peace between the Jews and Arabs, while undeniably "true," could never be "proven" or brought into being. In other words, Phil Matthews was dreaming if he felt there was a solution out there, unless it was one of unspeakable violence. While decent enough, he wasn't clued in.

"The solution," he said, "is to do what men do or to live somewhere else."

"And what do men do?" Phil Matthews was leaning forward with interest.

"They take offense when offense is given."

"I see. Very interesting." Phil Matthews consulted his watch then glanced at the interpreter. "I'm afraid that's all the time I have. But I'd like to see you again, if that's okay. There are still a few issues I would love to discuss."

"I will consult my family but it should be fine."

As the interpreter packed the equipment up, Mr. Matthews stood and shook Moussa's hand. He then approached the door and left, followed closely by the *Daffawiyya*. Moussa walked after them and watched them enter a car. When they started the engine and pulled away, both Matthews and the interpreter waved at him.

The exhaust hung in the air a few seconds then vanished completely. It seemed to symbolize Mr. Matthews himself: having asked his questions and done his bit for global justice, he was off and running to a brand new story. Truly he was from a different world.

Perhaps Moussa should have asked if he could come along.

CHAPTER THIRTEEN

"Do it! Do it! Do it! Do it! *Kol hakevod* Erez!"

Avi hated Feinberg, his phys. ed. teacher. Even if the guy was only trying to help, he was bully, a maniac, an out-and-out sadist. He loved making them jog five klicks. He liked to watch them strain at weights, fifty kilos, sixty, as much as they could handle. And he grinned when he asked for push-ups, pull-ups, sit-ups, crunches, curls, and squats. And now he was beaming as he watched them climb to their deaths.

"Do it! Do it! Do it! Do it! *Kol hakevod* Ilan!"

Feinberg had been a navy man once. He'd often describe an evacuation drill that his unit had been put through as part of their training. They'd been stationed on a cargo ship that carried tanks and artillery by sea. He and the rest of the crew were equipped with life vests, heavy knapsacks, and their M-16s. They lined up on the ship's top deck — it stood eight storeys above the water — where a platform led from the center deck to the stern's bulwark and beyond. At a signal from his officer — "one tough bird," Feinberg liked to say — each soldier was ordered to tear up the platform, jump as far as he possibly could, and crash into the water below. If he survived the collision, he had to swim his way to shore, return to the ship, and repeat the procedure.

And now he was exposing the class to a version of this hell.

He'd driven them to Hebrew U. Leading them to its Olympic-sized pool, with a number of duffel bags in hand, he took them over to the diving platforms and ordered them to strip down to their bathing suits. Several students emptied the bags, revealing full army uniforms, complete with heavy combat boots. There were also knapsacks stuffed full of junk: each one weighed maybe fifteen kilos. And to make things even more authentic, he'd brought along five disabled M-16s. How much did death weigh? Each gun was twice as heavy as that.

Their task was clear. In an attempt to capture the "drama" he'd been put through, Feinberg wanted them to dress in uniform, shoulder the equipment, and climb up to the highest diving platform. Once there, they would plunge into the pool below: a wrenching drop of "only" ten metres, as a way of achieving "mastery of self." He really was a sadist, Feinberg.

"Do it! Do it! Do it! Do it! *Kol hakevod* Yakovi!"

Dov and Itamar were ahead of him now. Like them, Avi was dressed in a sopping wet uniform (it had been used already by someone else) and was cradling one of the M-16s, whose dripping metal was cool against his palms. His stomach was tied in knots; his temples ached. He had always been a terrible swimmer, detested diving, and was scared of heights.

"Do it! Do it! Do it! Do it! *Kol hakevod* Dov!"

Itamar then him. He told himself how much he hated Feinberg, not only because he really did hate him, but because this hate would keep his fears from breaking loose. *Feinberg*, Avi thought. *So, he'd served with distinction in the navy? Big deal. Does that give him the right to torture students? Torture is against the Geneva Convention! Feinberg will go to jail if he's not careful. Look at him, with his muscles and killer's stare. Has he ever really killed someone? Or is that just a façade to disguise his own weakness? Hah! That's it! Feinberg is torturing us to hide his own fear, the goddamn chicken...!*

"Do it! Do it! Do it! Do it! *Kol hakevod* Itamar!"

Feinberg's hand was on his back, pushing him. Avi looked straight at him and realized the guy was no chicken. He'd stared down death and was asking them to do the same. "Don't let me down," he warned curtly, as his brawny arm propelled Avi upwards. Avi slung his gun over his shoulder and started to climb.

The first three metres were easy enough. The rungs were slippery beneath his boots, but he was moving quickly and cleared them in seconds.

"Go Avi!" Ilan shouted from nearby.

His rifle slipped and he had to sling it back. And the knapsack too was cutting into his shoulders. Just how many rungs had he climbed? It was best not to dwell on it and better not to look around, although it was clear he was high since the voices below were growing more distant.

His fear was coming hard at him now. It was like a hungry wolf that had been penned in a cage — no, a cardboard box. Its canines had punctured one side already and within a minute, even less, it would have broken out. There. Its head was visible and its jaws were gaping and its teeth were clacking together like shears. It wanted to feed on something juicy, his composure, his dignity, his self-respect....

He started humming "You'd Be So Nice to Come Home To." He was thinking of books and TV shows and movies (comedies, not action thrillers) anything to distract him from the insanity of that moment. And it was working. The wolf was slowly beating a retreat.

"Go Avi!" Ilan cried from ten miles off.

The last three metres were next to impossible. He was panting, there was water dripping everywhere, and he almost lost his footing. The smell of chlorine was overpowering and his uniform, knapsack, combat roofs, and rifle were pulling him down, to the cold, hard tiles, to disgrace and failure. His fear was back, but not as a wolf: it had assumed the guise of a skinny girl. Her dress was frilly, her arms were toothpicks, her knees were knobby, and her head was turned away; she wouldn't dare look a stranger in the face. Just as Avi was thinking he could tolerate this kind of fear, the girl whispered, in a high-pitched tone, *This is how they'll see you. When they strip away your exterior, you'll be left with this, the true Avi Greenbaum.*

He blanched. Her fingers were tightening round his ankles, undermining his drive to continue. She was giggling and singing and prattling nonsense. He started humming to drown her out: "*Hatikvah,*" the national anthem. Part of him wanted to scream with laughter.

"Go Avi!" Ilan cried again from the far side of the universe.

There. He made it. His lungs were heaving and he was sweating like a rat but he was at the top, he had cleared the last rung. And the nasty female brat was gone, like the wolf before her.

But now came the difficult part. He knew he shouldn't look down, but did anyway and the sight wasn't pretty. The ground was so incredibly remote. He couldn't jump, only an idiot would. If he didn't break his neck on landing, he would batter his intestines and die a slow, painful death.

His fear was back. Only now it wasn't a wolf or girl, but an old-fashioned, Hassidic Jew: he was dressed in black with an oversized *shtreimel*. He was stooped and cringing and wheezing slightly. And if a Nazi directed him to enter the "showers," he'd go obligingly and not lift a finger. He looked at Avi and said, *Just climb down.*

"Do it! Do it! Do it! Do it!" the voices started up from below.

He yelled at the *Hassid* that he was an Israeli, and Israelis were nothing like the *shtetl* Jews. They'd built a country and won five wars and made the desert bloom.

"Do it! Do it! Do it! Do it!" the voices persisted. They were like clubs and bludgeons in their attempt to make him jump.

He was so high up. And the only way back, the only way to escape, was to hurl himself forward, fly through the air, and drop and drop with all that weight upon him. To crash into the water, and, for an interval (that would last forever), to endanger everything that he held dear by surrendering any sense of control. It was the one and only way.

His fear was staring at him and it resembled … a teenaged boy who, while his brother sweated and manned the ramparts, was playing his music as he stretched out in bed. His fear was him. His fear was Avi Greenbaum.

"Do it! Do it! Do it! Do it!"

Do what? he wanted to scream at them. *What the hell did they want him to do?* But he knew. It was obvious.

"Do it! Do it!" they continued to scream as stood cringing on the platform. He was scowling when the realization dawned on him: Feinberg was no sadist but a passionate teacher. And the voices weren't bludgeons; they were actually a kind of padding. His friends were demonstrating that they would never let him down, that they would stand by him always … on one condition: he had to jump.

His legs were pushing forward. Even as his fear tried to wrestle him back, the wolf, the girl, the religious Jew, he was running, he was leaping, he was falling, falling, falling....

As he splashed and struggled against the water, and his muscles ached and his lungs caught fire, he felt released and lighter than air, for the first time since he'd last played soccer.

"... *Kol hakevod* Avi!"

"Harder! You can do better than that!"

"Do it! Do it! Do it! Do it!"

Moussa detested Omar, his phys. ed. teacher. The guy claimed he wanted to toughen them up, but he was a brute and always breathing anger. If you gave him fifty push ups or ran for an hour or lifted heavy weights, he would ask for more. "More!" he would yell. "So far you've given me nothing!" And today was no different; in fact it was worse.

"That's better! Dig deeper! Put your very soul into your blows!"

"Do it! Do it! Do it! Do it!"

He had been part of the Jordanian army, serving in one of its commando units. He'd often describe a "game" that he'd been put through. Once of his trainers had been a professional boxer, and as a crucial part of their combat training, they'd been required to go a round with this man — "An animal," Omar had called him. Although equipped with helmets and the thickest padding, these bouts had been hell. The hard part hadn't been taking the punches, though, never mind that his punch was like the blow from a hammer; no, the toughest part had been finding the strength to punch back. "Sure," Omar said, "it's no big deal to throw a punch; the real trick is to throw a punch with conviction." His own trainer had been merciless and taught by example: if you couldn't punch with feeling, he would take you apart. "He helped us find our anger," he explained. "And not anger which flies off in a hundred directions, but focused, distilled, purified anger, easily the deadliest force in existence."

"That's it! I felt that blow! Now you're getting the hang of it! Again!"

"Do it! Do it! Do it! Do it!"

They were in the school courtyard; Omar had brought boxing gloves and protective gear. After marking off a circle with a piece of chalk, he donned a pair of gloves and "invited" Amir to put the padding on. After punching the air a couple of times, he motioned his opponent to do his worst. A fiery kid, Amir lunged at Omar. While Omar easily evaded his blows, he praised

Amir for his "fire" and gave him some pointers. On rejoining his classmates, Amir glowed with pride.

"That's it! Wonderful! Do you see how your anger can be a thing of beauty? One more time!"

"Do it! Do it! Do it! Do it!"

It had been the same story with everyone else, Suleiman, Sami, Anwar, and now Mahmoud. Each had been able to channel his anger, an element that Moussa seemed to have in short supply — and he was next. The chest pad was strapped to him, the helmet with the grill was fixed to his skull, and two large boxing gloves were weighing down his hands. They looked almost comical, like the gloves a cartoon character might wear. But their leather was cracked and the left one bore a stain on its surface: blood. And then there was the terrible smell. It was a mix of leather and sweat and ... rage.

"Alright. Well done. Take a seat. Who's next?"

"Moussa," Amir said.

"Stand up Moussa. Show the group what you're made of."

With a sigh, Moussa climbed to his feet. He wasn't scared — there was nothing to be scared of. But he did feel ... empty. The fire he had seen in his classmates' eyes? The anger with which they'd launched themselves, recklessly, lustfully, against the snarling

Omar, as if they were Saladin's troops battling crusaders? This he didn't feel.

"Step into my home," Omar joked, motioning to the lines on the pavement.

He was telling himself that his *ab* was in jail, his *jadda* had suffered indescribable woes, Douad might never move back home, their store would be searched before long, and as he stood there waiting to be struck by lightning, bad things were happening throughout the PA, the Jews were bashing away at his people. With all these gnawing thoughts to fuel him, he still couldn't awaken his rage.

"Come at me!" Omar roared. "Do your worst!"

"Go Moussa!" Amir cried.

Moving forward, he struck with his right. Omar barely moved and he missed by a mile.

"That's it?" Omar asked, with a look of amazement. "That's everything you have? Hit me! Go on the attack!"

"Do it! Do it! Do it! Do it!"

The chalk lines on the pavement defined a separate realm. Even though Omar was only inches away, Moussa was alone, without a friend to help him out. And the only way back, the only way to escape, was to discover something deep within him that, until that very moment, had continued to elude him.

He closed in on Omar a second time and swung.

"That was even worse than before! Maybe this will help!"

Easily, almost effortlessly, his teacher struck and knocked him clean off his feet. For what seemed like a lifetime he flew through the air. He thought that this wasn't fair and that Omar was a jerk. This thought was quickly followed by the knowledge that the guy was going to hit him again, and again after that, until he had reduced him to nothing. Finally, just inches from hitting the ground, a voice inside was asking him why he would allow someone to insult him like this and wasn't he sick of feeling empty and denying himself entry to the ranks of men? Where was the virtue and profit in that?

When he hit the ground, his classmates groaned. Some were on the verge of jeering. Omar, too, was about to turn his back, as if Moussa weren't a worthy target, as if he was hopelessly lost to the group. He struggled to his feet. An unfamiliar heat was rising in him.

"Are you ready to strike for real?" Omar sneered. "If so, do your worst. Otherwise get out of this ring!"

"Do it! Do it! Do it! Do it!"

He lunged at Omar, with real spring in his step. He was prepared for another pathetic blow and was shocked when Moussa punched with such force that he staggered back a pace or two. More blows followed. Moussa was in a dream-like state, dodging and feint-ing and striking with rage, the delicious rage of a lion in action.

When he finally emerged from this state of posses-sion, and saw that Omar was practically beaming, and heard his classmates chanting his name, he felt more weighted than he had in ages.

Perhaps there was some hope for him yet.

CHAPTER FOURTEEN

Avi was flushed. He'd finished playing a Klezmer tune and the guests were going wild with applause. With tears in her eyes, Rachel thanked him for the song, saying she'd never heard anything so perfect. Even Dror was moved: his floating eye was fluttering in its socket. Meanwhile Dan was cracking jokes, most of them involving the suit he was wearing. His parents, for their part, were chatting together and seemed like a regular married couple: one would never guess they lived apart from each other.

Everything looked so clean and sparkling. The banquet room was filled with bright white chairs and tables set with gleaming cutlery. There were floor-to-ceiling windows on all four sides, which afforded a panoramic view of the city, from the Knesset to the downtown core.

Avi had moved over to the windows and was enjoying the view. He allowed his eye to wander east and to the desert not so far in the distance: the sun was setting and the sky was pink. The air about him was filled with smells: roast chicken, wine, perfume, and chocolate. A band was playing softly in the background, a medley of Israeli and American tunes, with bursts of conversation and laughter breaking through. And everyone was smiling, Rachel especially. For a moment Zohara came to mind. He'd thought about asking her to come to the wedding but, recalling their last talk, decided it was pointless.

"Can you believe Rachel's married?" Avi asked his brother, to distract himself from thinking of Zohara's smile.

"Not yet. I need more wine to get used to the idea."

"Mom's in tears."

"Of course she is. You know why?"

"Because her daughter's all grown up?"

"No. Because the speeches are starting."

Moussa threw himself into a chair. He'd been dancing furiously for the last half hour and was glad the band was taking a break. He had to rest if he was going to last all evening.

He pulled at his dress shirt. Like the rest of his suit it had been bought the day before and still felt somewhat stiff. He turned to the hall's picture windows and looked out at the city. The hall was on the top of a fancy hotel and the view was a breathtaking. To his left was the Dome of the Rock and, further west, the Jewish part of town, the downtown *midrachov*, the synagogue, and the Knesset — the place where the Jews passed their terrible laws.

"Did you get any cake?" Douad sank into a chair beside him. He was perspiring even more than Moussa and smelled of cigarettes, aftershave, and garlic. He was having the time of his life. Claiming Canadians were kind but far too reserved, he'd been maximizing his trip back home by visiting friends and staying out late. And from the time the groom had cut the cake with a sword, Douad had been dancing like a madman on a table.

"I've had three pieces," Moussa answered. "But I intend to have three more."

"Leave room for the *halawa*. It's not as good as Hannah's but it's tasty just the same. It's too bad she wasn't able to make it."

Moussa nodded and took in the room. While the crowd contained some two hundred people there

were lots of faces missing. Some relatives lived in West
Bank towns, like Abu Dis, Jahalin, and Wadi Qadum.
These places weren't far from the city, but they could
have been in Syria for all the Israelis cared. While some
guests had been admitted past the wall, others had
been turned back and forced to go home.

He tried to picture it, his relatives approaching
the checkpoint. Yusuf was among them, full of tales
about his stubborn mule, and Hanna with her *halawa*,
and Hamid who practised magic tricks. All would have
been dressed in brand new clothes and laden down
with food and gifts, and maybe the odd instrument.
They certainly hadn't carried any bombs. And yet,
after waiting hours, until the food had spoiled, they'd
been turned back for "security reasons."

"Some things never change," Douad said, lighting up a cigarette. "It's been two years since my last
trip home and still there's been no progress. But let's
think about more cheerful things," he went on, helping himself to a Jordanian nut.

"I can't," Moussa said.

"Why?"

"Because the speeches are starting."

— • —

They had heard from just about everyone, an uncle, Dan, Shosh, Dror, Dror's father, Dror's mother, and now their dad, the father of the bride, was speaking.

Mr. Greenbaum looked vulnerable as he stood up front with a microphone in hand. Although he didn't stick out physically perhaps, he did seem different from the Israelis.

"Thank you for coming to this happy affair. It's not every day a father has the joy of watching his daughter get married, especially to a *mensch* like Dror, and I'd like to briefly mark the occasion."

His father spoke conventionally for a minute, thanking the guests who had come from far away, and telling Rachel that her marriage to Dror didn't mean she could vanish from their lives; on the contrary, she was expected to stay in touch all the more. Then his remarks took on a very personal tone.

"I know a lot of you wonder," he said, fastening his gaze on a crystal chandelier, "why it is I live apart from my family. Some of you may have reached the conclusion that my wife and kids don't mean a lot to me or that I have no interest in the Jewish state. Without going into detail, I insist this isn't so. When I returned to Canada a while back, it was the hardest decision I've ever made. And ever since I've been lonely on my own and felt guilty that I couldn't bear things here.

"And that's the problem. I don't know what it is about this place, but it requires people to be exceptional. Some tough souls can live up to the call, and even thrive in the process — my wife's a good example of that; others can't. It became clear to me, after I'd lived here for a while, that I belonged to the second group and not the first.

"That being said, at my lowest moments, the thought always cheered me that I have three children living here in *Eretz Yisrael*, and that my efforts back in Canada help make this possible. When people ask me years from now what my greatest lifelong feat will have been, I will point to Rachel, Dan, and Avi, and perhaps to a new generation of Greenbaums, and say, 'Look there! Consider my Israeli family, heroes one and all!' And on that happy note, I'll let you get on with the meal. Please enjoy the rest of the evening. *L'chaim*!"

The applause was thunderous. Avi's tears were flowing freely. Under normal circumstances, he would have hid them from his family, from Dan especially who hated baring his emotions. But all of them were crying, his brother included; in fact, Dan was crying most of all.

— • —

Almost everyone had spoken: an uncle, Ahmed, Douad, Sayed, Sayed's father, Sayed's brother, and now it was their father's turn.

Tariq wasn't there in person, of course. Sayed was on the podium, holding a sheet of paper. After explaining to the guests that he'd received this letter in the mail, he called for silence and started reading in a sonorous tone.

"*As-salamu alaykum* honoured guests and kinsmen. For reasons far beyond my control, I cannot celebrate Alisha's wedding celebration with you. I want her to know, however, that I am sailing above al-Quds for joy because the man she is marrying this day is a fount of piety, discretion, fearlessness, respect, and, dearest to my heart, honour. May this couple enjoy many happy years together and bear many children who will dignify our families.

"To my other children, Douad, Ahmed, and Moussa. I acknowledge that I am a man of fiery temper and have subjected you to its flames too often. My criticisms might lead you to suppose that I take no pride in you and your achievements. If you think this way, the fault is mine. I never expressed satisfaction, when Douad was accepted into engineering, when Ahmed forsook his own education and ran our business with exceptional skill, or when my youngest son Moussa proved his mind is sharper than Saladin's saber. For my silence in the face of your talents, I am ashamed and humbly beg your forgiveness.

"When I die and the angels ask why they should open heaven's gates on my behalf, what will I reply to them? Will I speak of my own actions? These will only weight my soul with stones! Will I point to my prison term, as if the charge brought against me is meritorious in the eyes of God? I cannot believe the gates will open for such schemes. I will point to my children and ask the angels to admit me through their merit. I am confident that, when they hear my plea, a trumpet will sound and heaven will receive me.

"And so I end this wedding invocation. May all of us know only peace and joy all our days. *Fisehatak*!"

The applause was thunderous. Moussa didn't know what to do with his hands, he was squeezing them so fiercely to prevent himself from crying. His brothers helped him, Ahmed by seizing onto his left, and Douad by seizing onto his right, so that the three of them formed a lasting chain, one that time and distance would never corrupt.

— • —

"I leave tomorrow," Avi's dad told him. By now most of the guests had left and the staff was putting the room in order. The band had long finished playing and was packing their equipment away. Rachel and Dror were getting ready to leave — they were flying to Paris the following day. Dan was talking to Dror's relatives, and Shosh was giving Rachel last minute advice.

"You can't stay longer?"

"There's a trial back home that requires my attention."

"When will you be back?"

"As soon as I can. But maybe you can visit me when school lets out."

"That sounds great."

"I'll discuss it with your mother. In the mean time...."

His father couldn't finish speaking. Not wanting his son to see him in tears, he turned away and headed to the washroom.

For all his pride in his three children, he seemed the loneliest man in the world.

"What a night," Douad exclaimed. "I haven't had fun like that in years."

"Is Canada so boring?" Moussa teased.

"It is very boring. But that's why it's so pleasant."

It was getting on to 3:00 a.m. The pair were sitting on the penthouse terrace, surveying the city that lay at their feet. The guests had left half an hour earlier and the staff was returning the hall to normal. Ahmed was downstairs hailing a cab for their mother and *jadda*. Moussa wasn't tired at all, despite the hour and his constant dancing. If anything he felt energetic and was intent on watching the sun come up.

"But you'll be happy to come home?" he asked.

"Come home? Here?" Douad asked with an unlit cigarette between his lips. "Come back to searches and suspicions and threats? Come back to reports of people being shot and bombs going off in retaliation? Do you know how insane this is? Have you any idea what it looks like from outside? Canadians think we're out of our minds, Palestinians, Jews, Christians, Muslims. And they're right, we are crazy. We're insane, all of us. We spend our breath screaming for justice and we fight for justice and we bleed for justice, and all for what? More piles of bodies. Come home, to this? No. I will gladly call Canada my home if the immigration people accept me."

An ugly scowl had replaced his smile. He hadn't lit his cigarette and it dangled from his lips like a tooth wobbling loose.

"I couldn't even come home if I wanted to," he added. "By leaving I've lost my right to live in East Jerusalem. Can you imagine? Our family has been living in the city forever and the Israelis feel they can deprive me of my birthright. This city, this whole area which seems so peaceful in the moonlight, is plagued with insanity and I will not come back. I will not raise my children here. The soil isn't good enough. Once it was blessed but now it is cursed. I won't come home. I will die elsewhere."

He was crying. The tears were streaming down his cheeks and being plucked at by the wind — just a few among billions shed over the centuries. Wrestling back his own emotion, Moussa took the cigarette as well as Douad's box of matches. Lighting it, he gave it back to his brother. He also kissed him on the cheek, in an effort to compensate him for the future he'd been robbed of.

CHAPTER FIFTEEN

Avi inhaled deeply, hoping to relax his nerves. After weeks of practising, they were onstage at the Barbican Centre, where an organ filled the wall behind them and the audience was standing room only. The day of reckoning had finally arrived and they were competing in the youth orchestra contest. At Rivka's nod, they would play a Mozart Concerto, whose clarinet solo would shine the spotlight on him. Was he nervous? He was nervous. Was he ready? He wasn't quite sure.

"Give us an *A*," Rivka told Ilan. He swiftly played an *A* on his oboe and the woodwinds, Avi included, echoed the note. The brass section followed, then the lower strings and the upper ones.

As Avi listened to this groundswell of sound, his head filled with rich impressions. It had been a week since Rachel's wedding, yet he had taken in so many sights since then that it seemed more like a month had passed. For the last three days they'd toured the Tower of London, Westminster Abbey, the Parliament Buildings, the British Museum, Buckingham Palace, St. Paul's Cathedral, and other prominent places around London. Everyone had been dazzled by the city's grandeur, from its subway system to its sprawling parks. When they were in St. Paul's Cathedral, Zohara had said that as far as Christian landmarks were concerned, the city couldn't hold a match up to Jerusalem. And London wasn't as old, Dinah had added. While their remarks bolstered Avi's pride, they hadn't detracted from the magnificence around him.

They'd finished tuning and were awaiting a signal from the panel of judges. Avi pulled himself together. Instead of thinking about the sights he'd seen, he had to gear himself up for the piece that was coming. He focused hard. Could he play the solo without making mistakes…?

Something caught his eye. Turning slightly, he scanned the theatre. Something was up. At the back of the hall, on the highest balcony, a group had gathered and was fiddling with something: a series of sheets on which words had been scribbled. Slowly, they came into focus. Avi felt his spine turn to water.

FREE PALESTINE! one banner read.

ZIONISM IS RACISM! the second one proclaimed.

The audience was taking the spectacle in. There was a collective gasp throughout the hall, followed by cheers from a few scattered sections. Some people were yelling, "For shame! For shame" but their voices were drowned in a sea of murmurs.

"The sons of bitches!" Ilan muttered.

"Why are they targeting us?" Dinah groaned. "This is a music festival."

"Why?" Erez growled. "Because they're goddamn anti-Semites…!"

Everyone was whispering similar things. Only Zohara said nothing. Their conductor, for her part, was utterly calm. Having recovered from her initial shock, she tapped her baton and drew their attention.

"Enough of these distractions," she said. "If we're going to win this contest, we must play our best. Besides, we're Israelis. We know our conduct better than anyone else and have good reason to be proud of ourselves. Focus hard and show them what we're made of."

Her force of will was contagious. The fear that had started to gnaw at Avi gradually dissolved and he felt calm.

He was hanging on that signal. He was ready to play.

— • —

They were in Heathrow Airport. It was raining hard and flights were running late. The airport lounge was packed to capacity and passengers were sprawled out everywhere with their baggage. While Rivka went to inquire about their flight, the students were sitting and chatting together. They were mesmerized by the rain: it had been weeks since they'd seen such a storm and they loved watching the drops splash against the windows.

"I think we should have won," Zohara said.

"The Germans were strong. The Swedes were too." Dinah had admired the blonde, Swedish players.

"But their soloists sucked compared to Avi," Ilan pointed out.

"I wish we were staying," Erez said. "There's still so much to see, like Stonehenge."

"I wanted to see Oxford," Dinah agreed.

"And King Arthur's castle," Avi added. "Who knows? Maybe the rain will go on and we'll have to stay another week."

They continued discussing their impressions of England, when a man beside them spoke without warning. He was middle-aged and wearing a dark blue suit. He'd put aside *The Guardian* and was eyeing the group with a look of … disdain.

"Do any of you speak English?" he asked, with an upper-class accent.

"I do," Avi answered.

"Then maybe you can tell me what language you're speaking."

"Sure. It's Hebrew."

"That's what I thought. You're from Israel then?"

"That's right. We're musicians. We're part of a youth orchestra."

"So in addition to butchering people over there, you learn to play music? Not that it matters. You could play like bloody Beethoven and I wouldn't want you in England."

"What's he saying?" Ilan demanded, with a look of suspicion. Like everyone else, he spoke some English, but the man's accent was throwing him off.

"He's calling us murderers," Avi stammered in Hebrew, only to revert to English again. "I'm afraid you're exaggerating sir."

"Am I? I watch the news. I see what happens. Arabs are being beaten at random and shot to death on the slightest pretext. It's a disgrace. And as soon as anyone breaths a word, you lot go on about the Holocaust, as if you Jews were the only people to have suffered."

"I'm afraid it's not as simple as that...."

"It's not so simple! What cheek! That's exactly what I'd expect a Jewish thug to say. You know what I think? I think we should pull the plug on you, the sooner the better."

"What's he saying now?" Ilan and the others demanded.

"He says he would like to see Israel destroyed."

"The son of a bitch!"

"And I'll tell you something else," the man went on, rolling his newspaper into a bat. "I wouldn't let fifty million Jews pull the strings in the Middle East. We don't need you stirring up bad feelings with the Arabs."

"There are six million Jews in Israel," Avi tried to correct the man — in vain.

"Do you know why they bombed the London tube last summer?" The man was standing now, not listening to them. "Because of you. Because of what you're doing in Palestine. It's one thing to make a mess of your own country; it's quite another to let the rot spread here."

"He's blaming us for the terrorist attacks in London last year," Avi said in Hebrew.

"Why's he blaming us?" Dinah cried.

"Blame the terrorists!" Erez yelled in heavily accented English (but it sounded more like "blemsa tore his wrist").

"There you go, claiming it's not your fault. You're so predictable, the lot of you. Your army is vicious, your parents are vicious, and one day you'll be vicious, too."

"You are an anti-Semite," Erez said in English (it sounded like "Ewer aunty shemi" this time).

"Maybe you're drunk," Dinah ventured, in an accent just as heavy as Erez's. Her words came out sounding like, "may beer trunk."

"You are *efes*, zero," Ilan yelled. His accent was respectable.

The man flushed and raised his hand with the rolled-up paper, prepared to deliver someone a blow; Avi was the most likely target since he was sitting closest. But Ilan caught the bat before it landed. Erez and Itamar were standing too, and one of them gave the man a shove. Spying something dangerous in these boys, the man beat a speedy retreat and took safety in the crowd.

The group eyed each other, unable to believe what they'd witnessed. They were about to explode when they suddenly burst out laughing.

"Let's hope our plane is leaving soon," Ilan spoke.

"The sooner the better," Avi agreed.

— • —

"He hated us."

"Yes."

"I mean, he really hated us. I sometimes question our actions too, but overall I'm glad I'm Israeli."

"It doesn't show."

"No. I suppose it doesn't. I guess it's possible to be too critical. My parents focus on everything that's wrong; I guess we should talk about the things we get right."

"That's not a bad idea."

It was late. Their plane had left Heathrow well after midnight and the band had collapsed as soon as they'd been seated. Bothered by his reaction to the man, or rather, by his failure to react, Avi had hardly been able to sit. He'd kept praying for the flight to end and the plane to land on Jewish soil. To keep himself from fidgeting too much, he'd been studying the passing landscape below. Over Switzerland he'd admired the lights from various towns in the Alps. He'd been so taken by them that he hadn't noticed Zohara's arrival. It was only when she'd set some coffee down that he'd taken in her presence fully. If he hadn't had his seatbelt on, he might have hit the ceiling.

"I've never seen such hate before," she said. "What bothers me most is that he mentioned things I often argue. But my purpose is to build, whereas his is to destroy."

"It's rare to meet such people, thank God," Avi said.

"In the future I won't say negative things unless I'm prepared to say positive ones. That's a promise."

"Can you promise something else?" Avi asked.

"What?"

"That sometimes you'll ignore politics completely?"

"It's a deal," she agreed, smiling brightly.

"In that case, let's see a movie when we get back to Jerusalem."

He took her hand and closed his eyes. If it took weeks to reach Ben Gurion airport, he wouldn't complain.

CHAPTER SIXTEEN

For the third time in as many minutes, Moussa attacked the Israeli goal and smashed the ball as hard as he could. From the sidelines there was cheering amidst cries of alarm. And, for the third straight time, the Jewish goalie charged the ball and knocked it safely to another player. The cheers turned to groans, while the cries of alarm turned to screams of approval.

Frustrated, Moussa ran after the ball. How funny it was that he always felt anger when he played soccer.

"Challenge!" Rami cried. He was standing by the observation tower.

One of the Jewish players tried to mount an attack, but the ball flew off and rolled out of bounds. There was a pause as someone chased the ball, and Moussa used it to rest a moment. It was 43 degrees, and the sun was like a bludgeon. Like every player, Arab and Jew, he'd been running full throttle since the game had started. With the score tied at one apiece, both teams were frantic to clinch the match. Regardless of the heat and their state of fatigue, they would push themselves to the limit.

The spectators fuelled their desire to win. Whereas the first two matches had been private affairs, some two dozen people were now in attendance and watching events unfold from the sidelines. Half were Jews who'd been passing the field and were lured to the game by the sight of their flag — it was flying beside a Palestinian one. The Arabs had supporters, too: some labourers had spied their flag from a distance and, intrigued, they'd ventured over. When they'd seen their boys doing battle with a Jewish team, of course they'd stayed to offer their support.

"Look alive!" Rami shouted. "That forward will make a pass to his right!"

Moussa ran to stop the Israelis. But the center forward, instead of passing to the right, kicked to a player who'd appeared on his left. He then muscled past Amir and Sami, passed to the center who took stock of the field, then kicked to his right where a man lay open. This player had a straight shot on goal. The Jews were screaming, the Arabs were screaming, as the ball left his foot and….

With lightning speed, Abdul knocked it down.

"Score for us!" someone yelled in Hebrew.

"Score twice for us!" an Arab replied, in Hebrew too.

"Smash them!" the same Jew yelled.

"Drive them out!" the Arab cried.

"Over our dead bodies!" the Jew was snarling.

"That can be arranged!" was the Arab's reply.

Faisal passed to Moussa. He was about to set the next play in motion when suddenly everything came to a halt. A skirmish was taking shape to his right. An Arab worker was challenging a Jew. Both were yelling and gesturing fiercely. Some people wanted to intervene but others were telling them to keep their distance. Yossi ran across the field, screaming breathlessly in Hebrew and English. "It's just a game! Let the boys play!" Rami was also sprinting forward and yelling the same in Arabic and Hebrew.

But this wasn't just a game. Over the last few days things had heated up in Gaza and these events were fuelling people's fury. Hamas had been firing missiles into Israel. To stop these attacks, the Jews had shelled suspected sites in Gaza. One shell had drifted wide of its target and killed a family enjoying a day on the beach. *Tzahal* claimed that the blast had come from land mines — ones Hamas had planted in advance, no less — but the Palestinians didn't believe them. Four days later the army destroyed a van with missiles, and again they'd killed civilians in the process. In revenge, Hamas launched more missiles and a gunman opened fire on a highway, killing one Jew and wounding several others.

"This is crazy," an Israeli player half-muttered to himself.

"It is crazy," Moussa answered in English. His anger was dying now that they had stopped playing, but it had a little life to it still. This is why he added, "Things are bad in Gaza. It angers people."

Avi considered him. For the last hour his fear had left him, but it was flooding back because of this lull in play. He still felt bold enough to reply, "Things are bad in Gaza because your side keeps firing missiles."

Before their exchange could go any further, things were heating up on the sidelines. One bruiser had given another a shove and a full-fledged fight was about to break out. The Arab's meaty fists were curled; the Jew had assumed a karate stance. They were closing in and others were picking fights too....

There was a piercing scream.

"Gilead!" a woman cried. "What are you doing? Come down from there at once!"

"*Ima*! I'm stuck! Help me *Ima*!"

The tension faded swiftly as the crowd refocused on a different drama. A child had climbed the observation tower and was standing at its edge, near an old iron railing, a good five metres above the ground. His shirt was snagged on something: he kept yanking his arm but wasn't able to free it.

"Gilead! Help! My son is stuck!"

The woman had run to the foot of the tower and was rattling its metal door, heavy and dented and streaked with rust. Its huge steel panels were chained in place but the links had slipped, revealing a six-inch gap. The boy must've crawled through this space and made his way up the tower. The woman was trying to yank the door open, but as much as the chain shook, it would budge no further. She tried squeezing through the narrow gap but it was far too small for an adult to pass.

"*Ima*! I'm stuck!" The boy was crying.

"Gilead! Hang on! Help someone!"

The fight forgotten, the crowd was standing by the door, trying to figure out how the boy could be saved. Three men were wrestling with the heavy chain but, as hard as they strained, it still wouldn't yield.

"We need a ladder!" someone yelled in Hebrew.

"Or some cutters!" someone yelled in Arabic.

The boy was in hysterics now. He kept tugging and tugging but couldn't break free. His left arm was covered in blood.

"*Ima! Ima!*" he kept screaming.

"Do something!" his mother cried to the crowd.

People were on their cellphones, calling the police. Someone drove a van onto the field — it was the Jew who'd assumed the karate stance. Honking to clear a path for the van, he maneuvered it smoothly alongside the tower. Jumping from his seat, he scrambled onto its roof.

"Someone, get up here!" he cried, "I'll give you a boost so you can reach the tower!"

The Arab who'd been about to punch him climbed onto the roof of the van. The Israeli stooped and wove his hands together. The Arab used his hands as a step and, on the count of three, the Israeli hoisted him upwards.

"Gilead! Don't move! You'll only cut yourself further!"

The Palestinian reached as high as he could, cursing slightly as his skin scraped the concrete. His fingers just managed to catch the lip of the platform and, with a powerful heave, he hauled himself up, scrabbling with his feet.

"Don't worry Gilead!" he gasped in Hebrew. "I'm almost there, *motek*!"

A moment later he was beside the boy. There was a flash as he pulled out a large pocket knife and severed the boy's T-shirt in two — it had been hopelessly snagged on a vicious-looking hook. Using the fabric to cover Gilead's wound, he removed his own shirt and wrapped it round the child.

"What's happening? What are you doing?" the mother called up.

Without answering, the Arab crouched and gently steered the boy past the worn iron rails. He stroked his forehead and winked at him. At a signal from the Israeli, who had divined his intentions, he pushed the boy over the ledge, using his shirt as a makeshift sling. Clutching the sleeves as tightly as he could, he lowered the boy until he was within reach of the Jew. "You can let go," the Israeli called. Moments later the boy was being hugged by his mother.

The crowd applauded. Gilead and his mother were being ushered off the field where an ambulance stood waiting to rush them to a clinic.

Rami and Yossi declared the game a draw and agreed to meet in four weeks time. The crowd, too, was quickly dispersing, in a good-humoured mood now that the boy had been saved. The Jews and Arabs weren't friendly with each other, but the desire to fight had died completely.

Each side put its flag away, possibly out of respect for the other.

— • —

The Israelis were drinking sodas at the makolet. No one had spoken since they'd left the field.

"I know what's in that hangar," Ilan finally spoke, motioning to the building across the street from them.

"What?" the others asked.

"It's where they hide those people who think that one kind gesture can make a difference. The incident today doesn't change anything. Hamas is still firing missiles."

The others nodded and continued drinking.

The Palestinians were drinking soda on Al-Wad Road. They'd been deathly silent since they'd left the field.

"I know what's behind that doorway," Abdul finally spoke, motioning to the building across the lane from them.

"What?" the others asked.

"It's where they stow those idiots who think that one kind act can bring about peace. The incident today doesn't change anything. The Jews are still dropping bombs on Gaza."

The others nodded and continued drinking.

CHAPTER SEVENTEEN

Avi squeezed his knees together so his sister could get by. She'd gone to the kitchen to check the coffee and returned with a plate of cookies and chocolate. This was the first time she'd invited guests to supper and she wanted to get everything just right. And, in spite of the fact the chicken had been burned and the tomatoes had been hard and the rice had been soggy, the meal had been delicious. Although Rachel and Dror had been married just three weeks, their home had a nice, lived-in quality. It was tiny, yes, but cozy and hospitable.

"We'll have coffee at the table after the news," she said.

"Great," Dror drawled, motioning for silence. The TV played an awful scene. There had been a suicide bombing in Iraq, in an outdoor market packed with civilians. The footage showed bodies scattered at random: they looked like bundles of tattered rags. Three vehicles and a stall were in flames and firemen were fighting to contain the blaze, as medics were rushing around to treat the wounded. Dozens of people were in shock: a young boy was wandering around with a look of confusion, limping heavily and trailing blood. The announcer said the bomb was the work of insurgents who, in a video broadcast, swore to continue attacking until America quit the region.

There was silence as everyone absorbed these details. They were reminded of attacks they themselves had witnessed. Since their arrival in Israel, their city had been a magnet for violence: on buses, in cafes, in restaurants, and thoroughfares. One hundred and forty people had been blown to bits, and 1,700 had been badly wounded. And throughout Israel, 300 more had been killed, with thousands injured and traumatized for life. Most victims had been ordinary civilians whose only crime had been that they were going about their business, shopping for groceries, eating with their kids, or riding one of the public buses. At the height of the bombings, the Greenbaums had driven everywhere and tried to stay away from crowded places. And still there'd been some very close calls. One of

Dan's friends had been eating falafel, only to lose his leg to a bombing. And then there were the bombs that hadn't gone off, dozens and dozens of thwarted attacks, reminding Israelis that death was always possible. They understood the trauma in Iraq all too well.

Shosh and Rachel began debating. They raised all the usual points: how these attackers were animals, how they were desperate, how they were killing their own, how they hated the invasion, how the wall was a blessing, how it created anger, how these people were savage, how they were oppressed.

Avi thought he was going to go crazy. His fear pinned him to the couch, the endless arguing stirred his nausea (his sister's cooking didn't help), and the thought kept registering that this violence, this insanity, was what men imagined they had to do.

Mercifully, the item ended and scenes from a World Cup match flooded the screen. The sight of all those athletes in motion, their movements fast, precise, and graceful, was a welcome change from the previous footage. Dror and Shosh discussed the merits of each team. They were smiling now and reaching for the cookies, the heat from the first debate seemingly forgotten.

But still Avi felt like hell.

— • —

Moussa was sitting on his sister's couch, watching the footage with a raw feeling in his gut. They were eating at Alisha's for the first time since the wedding; Ahmed couldn't come because he was receiving new produce. The food had been tasty, exactly like his mother's — no wonder as Nadira had taught her daughter to cook. Sayed had been the perfect host, even if he proved a little too pious, punctuating his speech with religious expressions and referring too frequently to the sayings of the Prophet. No doubt these words were full of wisdom, but Moussa preferred his own brand of wisdom: mathematics.

They were drinking coffee and watching the news. The living room was tiny and they were all on the sofa, watching the horrific images unfold. There had been another bombing in Iraq. There were bodies everywhere, fires were raging, and people were screaming and tending the wounded. His mother and Alisha began to argue.

"If the U.S. just left Iraq, we wouldn't see these scenes," Alisha said. "The same way there would be no martyrs if the Jews were willing to give us some justice."

"But these bombers," Nadira answered, "are killing their own people, and Hamas murders Jewish women and children...."

"These people are doing their duty," Alisha said, mildly but with a note of rebuke. "They are dealing with the enemy and spreading the truth of our religion. They do so violently because it is the only language our enemies understand."

"But they kill the innocent," Nadira growled. "In their pursuit of justice they commit unspeakable crimes. I don't fault them for their anger, but I despise their methods. If they asked my sons to become *shaheed*, I would slam the door to my house on their faces. I did not raise my children so that they could kill and maim so viciously...."

Moussa thought he was going to go crazy. Whereas his mother and sister were flushed with anger, and Sayed's expression was one of stone, he was sitting there like a pile of spent ashes. This endless talk, too, about right and wrong as the TV bombarded them with scenes of innocent people dying, it had him spinning in utter confusion. And the thought kept eating at him that this violence, this insanity, was what men imagined they had to do.

Happily the scene changed suddenly and the screen was full of bodies in motion. Highlights from that day's soccer match were being played, and Moussa almost cried with relief as the TV provided him with scenes of life, and not half-charred corpses.

His mother, too, was smiling, and even Alisha seemed to appreciate the change, the heat from their argument forgotten.

But still Moussa felt like crap.

Avi was on a bus. The radio upfront was broadcasting the World Cup match. The bus was moving quickly, even on the turns, causing passengers to bump against each other: it was packed. He'd given up his seat to a frail, old lady and was swaying back and forth as the bus sped forward. He was wondering if he would be on time for his appointment.

Why did the man attract his notice? He was a small guy with non-descript features, dressed in simple clothes: dark pants, black shoes, and an overcoat. He was dark complexioned and neutral-looking….

Wait. The overcoat. That was what had drawn his attention. It was 42 degrees outside and the bus was sweltering. So why was he dressed in such a getup?

Avi studied the man with mounting tension. His eyes were glazed over and he was chanting softly. The coat was tight around his chest, as if something strained against its fabric. What? No, it couldn't be….

His eye traveled down the man's squat body.

There. Two filaments were attached to a remote he was gripping. They were running up along his wrist and into the sleeve on his coal black coat. With a thrill of horror he realized they extended up his arm, down his chest, and into the object that was stretching the coat's fabric. This was no simple object but....

He pressed a button to signal his stop. But the vehicle picked up speed and rattled by the next bus shelter. A woman waiting for the bus protested, little realizing how lucky she was.

Avi wanted to warn the riders. He wanted to reach the front of the bus and inform the driver they had a killer on board. But his mouth was dry and not a word would come out. And as much as he tried to push his way forward, in a way that wouldn't provoke the bomber, the crowd was no more yielding than a concrete wall.

The bomber suddenly looked his way. His eyes lunged straight at Avi's: they were pitch, pitch black and drained of mercy. There was no bargaining with eyes like these. If Death were a person, these eyes would be his. And they were shining with laughter: because Avi was scared, he wouldn't dare fight back. The bomber could take his time. In fact, he could postpone for an eternity and Avi wouldn't budge. But of course he had a schedule to keep. That's why he climbed to his feet and, pressing a button, shouted the words, "*Allahu al Akbar*!" There was a click, a roar, and a blinding light....

Avi screamed himself awake. His sheets were soaked top to bottom in sweat.

Moussa emerged from his bedroom. There were voices on the floor below and he thought he heard his mother crying. He descended the stairs two at a time, and, at the foot of them, saw his family had gathered: Ahmed, his mother, Alisha, his *jadda*, and even Sayed were standing in a tight little group. All of them had their hands tied behind them and were being led off by the Israeli police.

"What's happening?" he asked.

"Don't speak to them," a sinewy cop responded. "Under the state's anti-terrorist laws, I hereby declare them under arrest."

"On what charges?"

"Conspiracy."

"That's ridiculous! What evidence do you have?"

"The strongest evidence," the officer smirked.

"Bombs, like the ones you said my father was importing?"

"It's worse than that. Much, much worse," the officer snarled, while delivering a slap to Ahmed's head.

"What? Tell me!"

"You can't see it for yourself? It's clear to a blind man! These people are angry. They're burning with rage. And that's why we're going to lock them away. If we lock up all the angry Arabs, we Israelis will have nothing to fear."

The officer nodded to his men. Using their rifle butts they prodded the family — his mother, sister and *jadda* included — and drove them toward the front door. Just outside stood a fortified van, emblazoned with a Jewish star and with bars covering its doors and windows. As his family was herded past the threshold, no one looked back at him when he called.

The officer was about to leave, but Moussa ran to him and grabbed him by the sleeve. The man wheeled on him with a menacing look.

"We have a schedule to keep. Don't interfere."

"I won't. But I demand that you arrest me. Wherever they're going, I'm going too."

The officer drew back and grinned. He approached the door and practically roared, "He wants to come along! He wants to be arrested!" Hearing his words, his colleagues broke into laughter and his family started giggling, too. Soon Ahmed couldn't stand, his laughter was so strong, and tears were streaming down his mother's cheeks. Neighbours, too, were looking out their windows, their laughter adding to the general mirth.

The officer turned and shrugged his shoulders, stifling his laughter, as if to say, "Your request is utterly preposterous." Then abruptly he slammed the door and....

Moussa screamed himself awake. His teeth ached from clenching them so hard and, in his wildness, he'd overturned the table beside him.

CHAPTER EIGHTEEN

Avi ducked behind the divide. The balls were bouncing off its concrete surface and he could see red flecks painting the air. There was no way the shooter could actually hit him, but still he was firing, for the sheer thrill of it. And if Avi weren't careful, he would be pinned to the spot and a second "terrorist" would finish him off. He didn't want to look at his jumpsuit. The whole of it was steeped in red, a sign he'd been killed in every match that day.

"Avi! Over here! Crawl forward on your belly!"

This ordeal had been Ilan's idea. It was the first day of their summer break and he'd wanted to celebrate by playing paintball. Before Avi could say no, he'd phoned up guys from their soccer team and quickly won the lot of them over. They had assembled by the school and taken a bus to Talpiot. Some had been to the War-Zone before and, as a way of selling it to the rest of the gang, kept saying how realistic it was, how you really felt you were involved in combat.

That was the problem. Avi was thrilled with the jumpsuit and a plastic helmet with a full-face visor. When the clerk pulled out a gun, though, and snapped the CO_2 bottle on, he'd begun to feel a touch uneasy. And when he'd attached the hopper, which held two hundred paintballs, and fired a round to test that the weapon was working, he'd felt his fear grip hold of him as always.

Worse was to follow.

In the ensuing matches, he'd barely fired his gun. Whereas Ilan was burning to hunt the "Arabs" — they'd divided themselves into Golani and Hezbollah — Avi's instinct was to hide and duck, to retreat as soon as the enemy closed in. And when the time came to squeeze the trigger, he'd been so nervous with the cumbersome weapon that he'd fired at everything, except his target. Twice he had "killed" his own team members.

"Just crawl forward!" Ilan urged. "Four of them are bunched together. I can't move in until you give me cover. I'd ask Erez, but he's been taken out."

Taken out. Cover. He hated these words. He'd heard them spoken on TV and in movies, he'd watched as actors had killed and died, and he'd cheered when the hero, a strapping guy with wavy hair, had emerged victorious from his struggle with evil, wounded in the arm and limping, sure, but strong enough to bounce back in an action-packed sequel. But the realization had taken root over time that these words, when uttered, meant that death was near.

"Watch it! Yakovi's above us! He has a fix on our position!"

Paintballs exploded to Avi's right. Panic-stricken he crawled over to Ilan, who was cursing softly and shooting back. The guy in front was firing, too, and a pellet went whizzing over Avi's right ear.

"Through the window, quickly!" Ilan urged, motioning to a hole in a nearby wall of concrete. Desperate to escape, Avi flew through this hole and landed safely in the space beyond. Ilan didn't make it: as he'd tried to follow in Avi's wake, Yakovi hit him in the small of the back.

"That leaves just Avi!" Yakovi crowed.

"What about Aryeh?" Ilan demanded. "And I just saw Boaz...."

"They're both finished."

Avi ran the length of the space and reached a stairwell that led to the roof. Climbing it two steps at a time, he emerged at the top and searched for somewhere to hide. There was nothing. This was why they avoided the roof: it exposed you to fire from three different points.

What was wrong with him? Since the game had started he'd done nothing right. Okay, the first hit had been a surprise, the way it had stained his leg a deep crimson. His hair had practically stood on end and he was sure that he'd actually been injured. But the capsule had left a welt, that's all. So why had he kept flinching and bolting, instead of joining in his team's operations? Why weren't they bothered when the capsules hit, while he kept thinking it marked the end of the world?

Why? The answer was clear: his nerves were made of cheese, not steel.

"He's on the roof!" Dov cried, gloating.

"We'll finish him quickly," Itamar said. "He's trapped and won't put up a struggle."

"I'm glad he's not with us," Yakovi chimed in.

These last words struck Avi like a slap in the face. His posture straightened and his face turned red. These guys would never want him on their team. And who could blame them? He'd let them down since they'd started the game, always worrying about saving his skin instead of acting with the group in mind. If this game had been a combat situation, if the guns had been real, if the capsules had been bullets, Ilan would be dead and all because of him. What gave him the right to behave like this, to squirm at every suggestion of danger? Why was he allowed to give into his fear? Why was he behaving like an overgrown child when the man he would become was pleading to take over...?

Already he was running forward. To approach the roof, they had to pass a window at the top of the stairwell. If Avi hung from the edge of the roof, from a rail that was there to keep them from falling, could he lower himself and pick them off...?

Pick them off, his fear was saying. *There you go with that language again. And what if you fall? It's a three story drop and if you land on your head....*

Shut up shut up shut up, he shouted back at his fear, as he ducked around a concrete doorway, grabbed the rail, and lowered himself deftly. As if his limbs had rehearsed this maneuver before, his right foot found a purchase on the frame, his left foot steadied his swinging body, and his right arm brought his gun into position. The "terrorists" could only watch in horror as he riddled them with fifty rounds.

Nerves of cheese!

— •

"You missed him by a meter!"

"Did he notice?"

"Let me look…. No, he's still smoking. You try, Mahmoud."

Moussa frowned as he crouched behind a parked Peugeot. He and some friends were in the old bus station parking lot, just outside the city's walls. Cars were parked all over the place, many at irregular angles, and the boys were using these as hiding spots. They were armed with slingshots that Amir had constructed, from wire, leather, and heavy elastics. They could hurl a paintball a good fifty meters.

"Go on. You can do it," Amir said.

"Just don't let him see you," Abdul added.

"There!" Mahmoud cried, releasing the pouch with a twang.

"Did you hit him?" Amir asked.

"It seems unlikely. He's still smoking and looking up at the clouds."

"Maybe he's in love," Abdul suggested.

"Then we'll bring him to his senses," Amir sneered. "Here, let me try."

Anxious to enjoy their first day of vacation, the friends had met by Moussa's stall and wandered the quarter with their weapons in hand. At first they'd contented themselves with walls and doors: it had been fun to watch the paintballs hit a surface and leave a bright red mark behind. Amir had suggested they use paintballs and not stones because the capsules would be more accurate — and annoying. As an afterthought he'd added that they wouldn't hurt people

"Okay, I have him in my sights. I'm just verifying the wind resistance."

"The wind resistance," Mahmoud joked. "He thinks he's a sniper."

From walls and doors they'd graduated to more difficult targets. Moving into the Jewish quarter, they shot at flowerpots and panes of glass. They marked up cars and hanging sheets, and shot into any open window they saw, laughing at the thought of the mess they were making. "It serves them right," they kept repeating, as they fired into kitchens, bedrooms, and studies.

Moussa hadn't fired that much. It didn't bother him much to mark a door or wall, or stuff that could be cleaned without too much bother. Breaking things was a different matter, as was marking furniture with the crimson dye. As his friends laughed raucously about how the Jews would be scrubbing for the next three months, there was acid in their voices; it was absent from his. He also deliberately missed his targets, claiming he wasn't much good with a slingshot. His friends weren't exactly angry with him — anger was something they reserved for Israelis — but they did seem disappointed.

At one point they came across a dog and his owner. Amir hit the dog on its flank, causing it to yelp a little. While his friends laughed at the scarlet stain, Moussa complained that the dog was harmless and it didn't seem fair to attack it like that. Amir turned on him, snarling that the Jews had shot plenty of Arabs with bullets and not plastic capsules, and he didn't give a damn about some Jewish dog. The others agreed with him, mentioning friends who'd suffered because of the Jews. In their anger they might have started swearing at Moussa but, thankfully, the owner had spied them just then. Ordering them to stay where they were, he had taken out a cellphone and called the police. The four of them had rushed off and wound up in the old bus station, opposite a rampart where a guard was smoking. A Jewish guard.

"Ready. Steady. Fire!" Amir murmured, releasing the elastics with a look of satisfaction.

"Status report?" Mahmoud asked, like a soldier in some action thriller.

"The target is not neutralized," Amir joked bitterly. "Gunner Moussa, would you care to try your luck?"

"What's the point?" Mahmoud sneered. "His heart isn't in it."

"He has disgraced our sniper team," Abdul added, in a tone that said he was only half-joking.

For some reason their words touched a raw nerve. Why didn't he feel the same rage as them? Had his family been treated any better than theirs? Wasn't his father rotting in jail? Hadn't relatives been kept from the wedding? Hadn't his *jadda* been treated like dirt? What gave him the right to remain free of anger? Why was he behaving like an overgrown child when the man he would become was pleading to take over...?

Did he feel angry? Yes, no ... it was hard to say. But what difference did it make? Whether he felt it or not, he could still take action.

Shoving Mahmoud to one side, Moussa placed a paintball in the pouch of his slingshot. He'd noted that the weapon pulled a bit to the right, so he compensated by aiming a bit to the left. There was a breeze from the south, which he also had to consider. While his mind was calm and analytic, a fire flowed from his gut into his hands, allowing him extend the elastic further. The slingshot whistled like a bird of prey as the paintball hurried forth to work its business.

"Bull's eye! What a shot!" Amir murmured in triumph.

"You hit his neck," Mahmoud crowed. "He's rubbing it and … look, he's studying the dye."

"He thinks he's bleeding," Abdul said with a laugh.

Moussa was grinning. The target had been neutralized and his honour had been saved.

Avi was home. He was passing Dan's room. His brother was busy taking a shower, so he crossed the threshold and surveyed the room quickly. He spied what he was looking for: the M-16 stood over in the closet.

Avi hefted it. After carrying a paintball gun for six long hours, the M-16 didn't seem so heavy. He approached a window and held the rifle to his shoulder. He scanned the street and saw someone in the distance, a guy of maybe twenty, talking on a cellphone. He set him in his sights.

Could he do it? If an officer said this man was dangerous and ordered him to take him out, could he do it? Could he pull the trigger?

He forced himself to complete the picture. A deafening crack. The gun's recoil. The man glancing upwards with a look of shock, unable to believe he'd been shot through the heart. His fall to earth gurgling and with a red-soaked shirt. His last frantic gasps, a final shudder, his mother's anguish when she heard the news, his empty chair at the family table, and his tomb a reproach to the bastard who'd killed him....

Avi lowered the gun. He put it in the closet. It was only with a very great effort that he kept himself from puking all over.

His nerves were still of cheese, not steel.

Moussa was standing on the family's roof. He held his slingshot and a paintball capsule. A pigeon was roosting on a roof five meters off. It was sitting still and made an easy target.

He raised his slingshot and placed the paintball in its pouch. He drew back the elastic and steadied his aim, compensating again for the weapon's pull. He then forced himself to complete the picture. The elastic would snap forward and send the paintball hurtling. The bird would pitch a meter in the air and instinctively attempt to fly away, unaware its wing had been severed and blood was pouring from a gaping wound. With a stunned, near comical look it would slip from the roof to the street below. There it would shake for a couple more minutes until death, out of kindness, released its soul....

He lowered the slingshot and tossed it aside. It was only with a very great effort that he kept himself from puking.

If men carry tanks where they store their anger, much like tanks on the typical car, the needle measuring the rage in his tank was still pointing straight to zero.

CHAPTER NINETEEN

Moussa could think of nothing but soccer. All day he and his friends had discussed the World Cup play-offs, debating who they thought was most likely to win. Germany had beaten Sweden two days earlier, Argentina had dashed Mexico's hopes, England had eased Ecuador out, and Portugal had crushed the Dutch. There were three more games scheduled that day; Italy and Australia would be playing soon. As he wandered back to their market stall, having delivered all of his orders, he hoped Ahmed would agree to close early and hurry home to watch the match on TV. His excitement was so out of control that he almost hit a cat with his cart. Looking up from a discarded sandwich, the cat eyed him angrily and vanished down an alley.

Drawing near the stall, Moussa saw that Ahmed had taken out a radio and was listening intently. Three more people were listening in: Mustafa from the stall next door, two strangers, and, much to Moussa's amazement, Wasiim, the guardian of the mysterious doorway several buildings down the road. Moussa grinned: the Italy-Australia match had started. Looking at the men who were hanging on the broadcast, he imagined the fans across the globe who'd stopped their routines to tune into the broadcast: this was the magic of soccer. No matter who you were, whether rich or poor, Muslim or Jewish, the game offered something for everyone. It was the great equalizer.

He called to his brother from a short ways off. Ahmed motioned brusquely. The gesture wasn't like his brother and suggested that something else was up.

"Is something wrong?" Moussa asked, joining the group.

"We've killed two soldiers in Gaza," one man spoke. He was dressed in a yellow, short-sleeved shirt, had a chain around his neck, and stank of cologne. He looked very pleased but, at the same time, uncertain.

"We've kidnapped another," the second stranger said, a wrinkled gentleman in a jacket and *keffiyeh*. "The Israelis are fuming but it serves them right, considering they murdered the Ghaliya family."

"Hamas will teach them," Mustafa spoke up. He seemed nervous, the way he kept looking sideways, as if expecting to be pounced on at any moment. "Those guys are fearless and will burn the Jews' fingers."

"I thought you hated them," Ahmed asked, eyeing him sideways. "Last year, when they captured Gaza, you were raining curses on them for firing on Fatah. And you said you'd never bow to their *sharia* law."

"Look, I have problems with Hamas. But they're hammering the Jews, so how bad can they be?"

"My enemy's enemy …" Wasiim said quietly. Moussa discreetly glanced at him, taking in his rolling fat, sallow skin, and thinning hair — patches of dandruff covered most of his skull. The worst part was his eyes: they were very dark and very moist and had black, puffy pouches hanging beneath them. It would be hard to face such eyes directly: they projected a near unbearable sadness. His station by the doorway day and night, through summer and winter, would drive any man crazy. Still, for all his ugliness, his voice was deep and reassuring.

"This won't be good for business," the guy in yellow observed. "The Jews will open fire, people will riot, and again the tourists will keep their distance."

As if to prove this point, there was a rush of motion at the top of the road. Rounding a bend some fifty metres distant, a knot of heavily armed soldiers appeared. There were lots of them and they were marching swiftly; they had a no-nonsense air that forced pedestrians to step aside. A number of merchants were packing up their wares, just in case the scene turned violent.

Once they had passed the stall, the man in yellow spat. The four men started their discussion again: how quickly would the Jews open fire in Gaza and how aggressively would Hamas respond? Their voices were rough, impatient, and inflamed as they expressed how each would like to deal with the Israelis. Hearing their anger but unable to reflect it, Moussa felt himself contracting — and a moment ago he'd been so cheerful! He had to escape their collective rage before they discovered that his own anger was sleeping.

Then it hit him: if Wasiim was standing in front of the stall, who was watching over his doorway…?

He snuck away from the group, keeping an eye on Wasiim. He was so engrossed with the talk around him that didn't notice as Moussa crept off. Moussa rounded a narrow bend; safely out of sight he started running full tilt to increase his lead time over Wasiim, and praying that the "guardian" had forgotten to lock up. There, the doorway was visible and….

It was yawning wide open!

He slid up to it, panting slightly. Determining the coast was clear, he inhaled deeply and crossed the threshold. He grinned as he imagined himself solving the mystery and describing to his friends the stuff cluttering the space beyond: mouldering produce, pots and pans, old TV sets, and half-broken souvenirs.

The space inside was lit by a single bulb — it couldn't have been stronger than thirty watts — and it took him a minute to adjust to the shadows. He was expecting a dank, dusty room but the air was dry and nicely chilled. There was a faint smell; it was sweetish, yes, and only slightly unpleasant.

The space itself was bare. There was no furniture, no stock, no register, nothing. The walls displayed no shelving but.... How odd: they were covered in shirts. Was he mistaken? No, they were certainly shirts, hundreds of them. So that was the great mystery? Wasiim was in the clothing business?

He was about to turn away when he started thinking. If Wasiim was in the clothing business, why didn't he exhibit his wares outside instead of storing them in the dark like this? And where did he keep his extra stock? And, was it his imagination, were these shirts secondhand? He leaned in closer. Yes. How weird. The shirts were ripped, torn, and tattered, some of them beyond all hope of repair.

And some of them were horribly stained — no, all of them were, without a single exception: each exhibited gross red blotches that....

He sprung back in horror and practically retched. It was blood! Each shirt was steeped in blood. Their former owners must have met with violence, gunshots by the look of it, and maybe worse. Who ... what...?

He shivered as the truth struck home: this wasn't a store; it was a shrine. The space was dedicated to the sad, sad souls who'd been shot by the Israelis or blown up by their missiles. Wasiim had somehow acquired their shirts and tacked them to his walls to do these poor ghosts justice.

Moussa viewed the shirts with respect, sorrow, and mounting horror. He couldn't catch his breath. The space paraded too much tragedy and sadness and it was squeezing the air from his lungs. His feet were carrying him backwards. He couldn't take it in all at once: the bloodshed, the suffering, the courage, the folly. And the anger. The shredded fabric with its rosy stains conveyed, even in death, a rage so grim and deadly that it was practically setting the walls on fire, causing the earth to tremble.

He started. The shirts, they were moving! Despite the tacks fixing them in place, the T-shirts were shuddering as if still reeling from the volley of shots; the dress shirts, too, were reaching out with their sleeves as if to touch him and prove the extent of their wounds. "Look! Look!" they seemed to be saying. "Do you see what we have suffered? Do you see what we have given and what was taken from us?" They were closing in on him, one and all. The holes and tears and lurid stains were, above all else, an accusation. The shirts were accusing him. What did they want?

As if he didn't know.

"I understand," he gasped, fighting back his tears. When still they shook and shuddered and flinched, he practically shouted: "I'll do it! I'll fight. I won't let you down."

He turned and fled. Running as fast as he could back home, he expelled the room's foul fumes from his lungs and kept blinking to clear his eyes of its horrors.

But wherever he looked, he was confronted with blood.

He was on the roof. He had the slingshot in hand. A short distance off a pigeon was roosting. He slipped a paintball in the pouch. Drawing the elastics, he took aim. Moments later the bird fluttered slightly as the paintball struck it full in the chest, passing through its fragile body.

The bird heaved a couple of times then stopped. It had been graced with life and now this blessing was gone. But Moussa too had been transformed. He had been innocent once; he was no longer. Who was he to be innocent? Why should he be free of rage?

If that bird had been a Jewish soldier? If the slingshot were a gun? If he'd been told a Jew had fired on his brothers, even if only to protect his own? Could he squeeze the trigger? Could he take human life?

A feather blew towards him and he smiled grimly.

CHAPTER TWENTY

Avi rushed off from Ilan's place, where they'd been watching the England-Portugal game. The match was only halfway done and so far neither side had scored, but his mother had called and told him to go home. Dan had contracted some sort of bug and was lying in bed, sick as a dog. She had some ministry papers to drop off and didn't like the idea of leaving Dan home alone. She wasn't normally the coddling type, so Avi knew he should get home quickly.

In some ways it was lucky Dan had taken ill. The Gaza campaign had entered its fourth day and the situation was looking bleak. During commercial breaks for the England match, Ilan had switched to the Israeli news, opening a window on a very different world. Instead of a stadium with emerald grass and cheering fans, they'd

been faced with scenes of ruination. Hamas was launching missiles from all over and that meant there were
tons of possible targets: apartment blocks, offices, stores,
schools, markets, mosques. The air force was trying to
keep casualties to a minimum, but even so it had hammered the region and the effects were really starting to
show. There was smoke everywhere and burnt out cars
on the roads. Gaping craters appeared at random: the
aftermath of missile strikes and constant bombing. The
earth looked like it had been set on fire. An electrical
station had been pounded flat: its metal frame was broken and its complex guts had been blown to hell. And
the people. The women were either crazed with grief
or screaming words of hatred and rage. The men were
either rescuing victims or opening fire on the Israelis.

The army was calling up more and more troops.
Until he'd fallen sick — under-cooked chicken was to
blame — Dan might've been be added to their number. Never had under-cooked chicken been greeted so
warmly.

He was still five minutes away from home. He was
hurrying past the field where his team had played the
Arabs when he paused at an unusual sight. The hangar that he'd skirted so many times before, that stood
between his street and the field and was locked day
and night, in summer and winter? For the first time

ever its gates stood open. Not just the gate facing the field, but the one on his street as well.

He hesitated briefly. Should he…? If a place was locked, people liked it that way — and by people he meant the state authorities. But he *was* in a rush: what if Dan wanted water but was too weak to stand? The hangar was all of eighty metres long and could be crossed in a matter of thirty seconds. Besides, if anyone had seriously wanted to keep people out, they wouldn't have kept the gates wide open and would certainly have posted NO TRESPASSING signs. Yet there wasn't a single sign in sight and the guards on duty seemed to have excused themselves. Even though his fear was warning him not to, Avi thrust it aside and ducked inside the structure.

It was only after a dozen steps that he started wondering what its purpose was. The answer seemed easy enough: it was a depot for surplus public buses. It did surprise him a bit: he would have thought any such depot would be near the station on Jaffa Road; and, through all the time he'd lived in Musrara, he'd never seen a bus leave or enter this depot. Maybe they travelled late at night, unless there was a tunnel he wasn't aware of.

He paused to study a bus more closely. It wasn't operational: it was missing its front doors. Was it undergoing repair perhaps…? Yes. So the place wasn't a depot but more a garage: that explained why the next bus over was dented in front. Well, not dented so much as brutally hammered, as if someone had....

His blood froze. It wasn't. It couldn't be that.

But the evidence was indisputable: that's what it was.

This wasn't a depot. It was a bus graveyard. There were over thirty buses, and each had suffered its share of violence. Some were riddled with bullet holes; others were dented from the outside in, most likely by a vehicle that had acted as a battering ram. And then there was a third class. The buses in this group verged on the obscene. Their outsides had been hammered open by what must have been a giant filled with implacable rage. The seats, poles, and windows had been reduced to tangles of indecipherable matter, as if the giant had crumpled them in his meaty fists. Still not satisfied with the destruction wrought, the giant had belched gas over the fixtures, struck a match, and set the mess ablaze, so that everything was charred and melted together.

Avi had to remind himself to breathe. The remnants of these vehicles were bad enough, but he couldn't stop thinking about the passengers who'd been seated inside. If brute matter could be so viciously altered, imagine the effect on the helpless victims. Their skin, their bones, their organs, their beauty, their talents, their prospects: all were gone, all had dissolved, all had vanished in a flash of rage that murderers had confused with the will of God.

He was shaking. He was sweating. His breath wouldn't come. And the buses, they were closing in. He could have sworn they'd somehow inched themselves closer. Yes, a headlight flashed. A phantom horn sounded. Figures were waving from the smashed-out windows and had something they wanted to share with him. They wanted to grab him and shake him senseless, as a way of impressing him with the weight of their losses, the sweetness and innocence that they'd been robbed of, and all because they had ridden a bus.

"Alright!" he yelled. "I understand." But this wasn't nearly enough for the buses: their engines started and their outlines inched closer. The toxic fumes from their phantom engines wafted about him and cut off his air.

"I'll do better!" he cried. "I won't let you down!"

With this promise made, he took to his heels. He escaped the hangar and was breathing freely and rubbing his ears. He was trying to hear the sounds around him, but the only noise confronting him was a thunderous explosion and the cries of people dying.

— • —

"You're very quiet. Is something wrong?"

"Nothing. Can I get you something? Soup? A sandwich?"

"Don't mention food! The mere thought of it will send me running to the bathroom. Although … I could maybe handle some juice."

"Don't move. I'll get it for you."

"I'm not going anywhere. And I wonder how this game will end. I suspect they're headed for a kick off."

"You're probably right. I'll get that juice."

"There's a glass of it beside my bed."

"Sure."

Avi walked into his brother's room. He got the juice and was about to leave when he spied the M-16 in the closet. Exhaling sharply, he put the juice back down. He lifted the rifle, surprised to discover that it was lighter than before. He approached the window and peered outside. A man was on a bench reading the paper; he was wearing earphones. Avi raised the gun and brought this man within its sights.

If an officer informed him that this man was a threat? If he were told this man was strapped with explosives or armed with a gun that he would use in the ongoing efforts to attack the Jewish state? If the

218

officer ordered him to kill on sight? And if he knew, before he squeezed the trigger, that some mother's son was going to die and he, Avi Greenbaum, would be the source of her grieving. Would he pull the trigger? Would he?

Without a moment's hesitation.

CHAPTER TWENTY-ONE

July 6, 2006 (Thursday): 11:25 a.m.

"Alright, that's everything. We can start when you're ready."

Phil Matthews looked up from his equipment and smiled. When he had phoned a week earlier and asked if they could meet, Avi hadn't been enthusiastic. What use would another interview serve? Phil Matthews wanted to ask him questions, but he was starting to think that no answers existed, that one could talk and nothing would change. For him, at least, there was only one issue: was he ready to do what men do? He was finally confident the answer was yes.

It didn't help that there was feedback from their last talk together. Some comments had been positive, most of which had come from Jews. Half had been neutral: refusing to condemn one side or the other, these listeners had stated the obvious truth that peace was more attractive than war. And then there'd been the remaining quarter (and a lot of these had come from Jews as well). In a word, these critics were brutal. They claimed he was spouting propaganda, that he was willfully blind to his government's crimes, that he was consuming resources that belonged to the Arabs, and that the CBC shouldn't play such twaddle since it only served to legitimize Israeli aggression. As if these Canadian "experts" knew better than the Israelis themselves.

"Shall we begin?" Phil Matthews asked.

"Sure."

"Great. I'm here with Avi Greenbaum again, in his apartment outside Jerusalem's Old City. We spoke seven weeks ago and I've returned to ask a second round of questions. Before we get to them, would you like to respond to our listeners' comments?"

"Not really."

"Oh? Why's that?" Phil Matthews was surprised.

"Because they don't know what they're talking about. When they speak of propaganda, they don't know how our media works. When they say I'm blind to the situation, which is comical to say the least, they're claiming to have a better view of the facts, never mind that they live halfway across the world. And when they say I have no right to the land, I guess I should ask them what they're doing in Canada — unless they're all Aboriginals, that is."

"I see…. Can we talk about developments since I spoke to you last?"

"Sure. My sister got married — the wedding was great. My father came to visit, but he couldn't stay long. I went to England with my classmates where our orchestra came in third in a youth orchestra competition. I finished school with pretty good grades and I believe I actually learned a lot this year, especially these last two weeks. And the World Cup series has been intense so far. And there you have it."

"What do you make of events in Gaza?"

Avi almost smiled here. When Phil Matthews had asked him what was new, he didn't want to know about this normal stuff; he'd been angling for something a little more compelling, whether friends he knew had either killed or been killed. That's what the country meant to people: their story wasn't about love and family, the rewards of hard work, or the pleasure of music, priorities that lay at the heart of their activities. No, the story they were interested in had death at its core.

"Let me see. Hamas hit us, so we hit back at them. They hit us again, so we returned the favour. They hit us a third time, so we sent in our jets. We don't like it. They don't like it. The UN has also voiced its disapproval. And there you have it. What else is new?"

"The media faults Israel. Canada's *Globe and Mail,* the *Boston Globe,* the *Washington Post* and most European papers. How do their impressions make you feel?"

"I don't feel anything. I don't care what they write. Let them choose sides however they see fit. But if they do choose Hamas, they're sending a strong message."

"What sort of message?"

"That they prefer backwardness to modern ways. That they support a system where you can't speak your mind, where women have no freedom, and where religion counts for everything. Good luck to them, that's all I can say."

Phil Matthews was eyeing him strangely, as if Avi had changed since the last interview, to the point that he was a completely different person. And in some ways he was. Being prepared now to do what men do, he had decisively left his boyhood behind and hadn't time for anything he considered nonsense.

"Some people might say that Israelis are touchy," Matthews went on. "They feel that as soon as they say something bad, Israelis condemn them as anti-Semitic. Can you comment on that?"

"Some criticism's fair. Some is just awful. Take my brother, for example. If someone says he's a killer because he's a member of *Tzahal*, well, either he doesn't know my brother, or he doesn't understand the situation, or he's anti-Semitic. The problem is, people don't know us. They see a couple of TV broadcasts, the images are awful, and suddenly they're experts. They should speak to us before they point their fingers. Otherwise their opinions are weak, even hateful."

Phil Matthews paused. He was still digesting Avi's new gruffness. Avi wished he would leave. He wanted to kick a ball with Ilan, or take Zohara out to a movie, or play some music, or hang with his friends. This interview was a waste of time.

"Let me ask you this." Avi rolled his eyes. More questions. "Whether critics are acting fairly or not, they're interested in Gaza and the footage is upsetting. What can you tell them that will set things in a different light?"

Avi mulled this question over. Despite his seemingly dismissive remarks, events in Gaza did worry him. When he saw a missile demolish a building, he could easily picture the horror it wreaked, the ghastly sounds, the shrapnel flying, the raging pain, the blood all over. When he saw bodies littering the streets and images of parents burying their babies, or kids squatting beside a dead parent, howling with a sorrow that would never leave, he had to close his eyes. The pictures were so wrenching. Were they right to react with such deadly force? He could defend his brother and he could defend Israelis, they too were bothered by the bombs and missiles and tried to minimize the pain inflicted, but the question remained: were they acting justly? People were dying because of their actions, not just terrorists but innocent folk, as well. And Phil Matthews was entitled to ask whether anyone has the right to cause such anguish. Granted Hamas wanted to destroy the nation, but did this allow the "good guys" to blow them to pieces?

He didn't know. No one did. The generals, the media, the rabbis and mullahs, the right wing, the left wing, no one knew. You could consult the Torah, the Koran, the New Testament, Gandhi, Einstein, the Dalai Lama, the nicest people, the smartest ones, the church-going people, the secular ones, and still you wouldn't get a concrete answer.

But Israelis had to act. That was the problem. They hadn't the luxury to mull things over, not when rockets were hitting their cities, soldiers were being kidnapped, and bombs were exploding. Right or wrong, they had to act. And in acting they advanced with a

NICHOLAS MAES

limited perspective and would have to take the blame
if the results were ugly. If they blew up buildings and
electrical stations, right or wrong, they would have to
face the possible fact that they had cut young children
apart in the process, even though they could truthfully
argue that it was done only to protect their own families. This is what it meant to do what men are forced
to do.

But these strictures applied to Israel's harshest critics. They too had a limited perspective. If they thought
there was a simple solution, that the problems could
be solved once and for all by granting the Palestinians
a state of their own, maybe they were right, maybe
they were wrong. But who would pay if they were
mistaken? Whose homes and cities would be attacked?
And the critics weren't entirely honest. They liked to
downplay Arab aggression, the hatred and ignorance
often dogging the "victims": in their eyes they were
innocent and could do no wrong. These critics tended
to neglect, as well, the grinding effects of being threatened daily, on buses, in restaurants, or when shopping for groceries. Did they think that Israelis liked
going to war? That they experienced a thrill when they
were called to arms, that they relished the prospect of
exchanging fire? This wasn't true of anyone he knew,
and no song of theirs, no book of theirs, no poem of

226

theirs, no film of theirs glorified war in any way. And finally, these critics were blind to the fact that Jews were always assessing the cost of statehood; whether the dream of Zion, which had nurtured them in exile, was worth the soul-destroying price, the beatings, the arrests, the endless suspicions?

They are lucky, he thought, *Western people. They don't face the same tensions as us and their men no longer have to do what men do. Their choices don't involve them in life and death issues. They are rich. They are privileged. And while they want to judge, and feel obliged to judge, their judgement, like ours, will be inherently flawed.*

Phil Matthews was waiting.

"My dad used to tell me bedtime stories," Avi said. "Fairy tales like the 'Three Little Pigs,' 'Cinderella,' 'Snow White,' and 'Jack and Beanstalk.' He liked to mess with the regular plot lines and tell the stories from the villain's point of view, from the ogre's and not Jack's, or from the witch's and not Cinderella's. It was funny because I would cheer for the villain, even if the villain was up to no good."

"You're saying things are a matter of perspective?"

"Yes. If you see things from our angle, missile attacks, suicide bombings, a kidnapped soldier, troops shot down, you'll think we have every right to bomb. But if you see it from the Arab side — the occupation, civilian deaths, poverty, beatings, and daily arrests — well, you might be tempted to argue their cause."

"So the Israelis aren't right and the Arabs aren't wrong?"

"Of course not," Avi said with some surprise. "No Israeli I know thinks the Arabs are wrong. I mean, we think their suicide bombers are evil, and Hamas is cowardly to hide behind women when they shoot their missiles; but we understand why they would want their own land. If it were merely a matter of right and wrong, the situation wouldn't be nearly as crazy."

"I'm afraid I have bad news for you. Most people think it does involve right and wrong. And when they're asked to choose sides, they often side with the Arabs."

"It must be nice to have such certainty," Avi said sarcastically. "Still, it makes no difference. It's not my job to set your listeners at ease. Our job, in Israel, is to protect ourselves and, for our sake not for your listeners', to deal justly with others."

"But can you judge what is just? That's the ultimate question."

"We can judge as well as anyone. And if we're not fit to judge, then no one is."

The interview lasted a few minutes longer. But the hard questions had been dealt with and Matthews moved on to less troubling stuff: his plans for the summer, whether the war in Gaza had affected his routines, and what he was planning to study next year. He then switched his recorder off and packed his stuff away. A moment later Matthews was descending the steps, having thanked Avi repeatedly for speaking his mind.

As Avi watched him drive away, he felt resentful, hostile, and somehow abashed: he wasn't used to speaking so directly.

But at least his fear was a thing of the past.

CHAPTER TWENTY-TWO

July 9, 2006 (Sunday): 1:25 p.m.

"Okay, we can start. And thank you for the tea. It's refreshing on a day like this."

"It's my pleasure," Moussa answered with a frosty smile. When Phil Matthews had phoned and asked to see him again, he had wondered what use this talk would serve. Why was this journalist interested in him? Did the man have no family of his own to look after? Perhaps he was bored with his life in Toronto and was there to give himself a bit of excitement? Unless he had taken his freedom too far, like so many others who came from the West, and wanted to see real traditions in action. Whatever his excuse or motivation, Moussa had better things to do with his time.

"Rashid will translate so don't hold back," Phil Matthews pointed to the *Daffawiyya* who, if it was possible, looked even thinner than before. "First of all, the usual introduction. I'm here with Moussa Shakir again, a resident of Jerusalem's Muslim Quarter. Let's start with the comments our listeners sent in. You've had a chance to look at them. What do you think?"

Moussa grimaced. While half of the comments had been warm and friendly, others had been negative. Some had pointed out, on the issue of freedom, that Hamas was more controlling than the State of Israel. Women couldn't act as they pleased, Gazans couldn't speak their minds freely, playing music was out of the question, and many books were strictly forbidden. So who was Moussa to blame the Israelis?

Others argued Arafat, former head of the Palestinian Authority, was really to blame. Not only had he helped himself to a billion dollars of outside funding, he had incited terrorists to kill Israelis. And when one considered the history of Arab violence, from the Ma'alot killings to the 1972 Olympics, the Israelis had been comparatively kind and forgiving — or so Daniel Cohen of Montreal had written in.

"I have little to say."

"Really? Don't tell me you agree with these people's opinions."

"It's not that I agree with them. They have one way of seeing things; I have another. We are like parallel lines and have no point of intersection. At least with Hamas — to address some listeners' concerns — I have an important point in common: we are all Palestinian and wish to escape Israeli rule. What happens next, how we deal with religion and our situation, that's our business and no one else's. Mr. Cohen, you live in Montreal. I take it you don't want to live with Israelis, either."

Phil Matthews looked bewildered, as if he'd been expecting to interview one person, and another had shown up. And maybe that was true. Now that he had tapped into his anger, he had turned his back on his childhood forever. And with the abandonment of childhood came a more sombre view of the world.

The *Daffawiyya* felt it too. He seemed to see there was more to him than the spoiled child he had been before. His tone was much less chiding now, as if he appreciated Moussa could do what men do.

"We haven't seen each other in a while. Can you tell us how things have developed since then?"

"My sister got married and the wedding feast was wonderful, even if the Israelis kept some families from attending. I saw my brother, who lives in Canada, and my father even wrote us a letter from jail. Our shop hasn't been searched — that is always positive — and business has been good these days.

"What about Gaza?"

Moussa had to smile. If the Palestinians had been rich, with a state of their own, would Phil Matthews have been interested in their thoughts and feelings? If there'd been no wall, no refugee camps, no road-blocks, no closures, no Deir Yassin, would Canadians have even known that Palestinians existed? Of course he was grateful for their intervention: any pressure on Israel was fine by him. But it was a funny way to treat a population, to befriend them only when they needed something and not when they could stand up on their own two feet. This wasn't friendship; it was charity.

"Hamas' rage rolled out of control. And when the servants defied the master, the Jews cracked their whip."

"But was this wise or necessary? If Hamas knows Israel will make use of its jets — and they must do something to combat those missiles — why would they want to trigger the storm? It only serves to endanger their own women and children."

"Maybe they feel they must keep up the pressure. If the Jews enjoy the fruits of peace for too long, they will never be willing to give us a state. As my brother likes to say, a tree must be shaken if the fruit is going to fall."

But even as he spoke, Moussa had his doubts. When Hamas had taken over Gaza, terrible stories had trickled out: of beatings, shootings, and men pushed from windows; of pleasures banned and freedoms removed in the name their unsmiling God. Hamas reminded him of little kids who put beetles in jam jars and neglect to punch holes in the top, preventing air from seeping in. If he were living under their rule? They would take away his books and films and maybe even his soccer ball and force him to memorize tracts from the Koran. They would beat him if he broke the rules and would expect him to beat "sinning" Muslims in turn. His own sister represented what he could expect: before meeting Sayed, she had not been so traditional; now she followed his every injunction and allowed him to dominate her thoughts and speech, to the point he determined the people she could speak to.

And what about the violence? While he admired Hamas for attacking the Jews, he often found their rage excessive and their tactics unacceptable. Could he praise a movement that urges its members to let bombs off in public places and reacts ecstatically when the death toll mounts? Could people be trusted who celebrated death and preferred it to life's simple pleasures? Phil Matthews certainly had a point: their attack on

Israel had been reckless, never mind it was bold. And because of this recklessness, innocent people would die. And to hide behind women when they launched their missiles, hoping the Israelis wouldn't dare shoot back? How could anyone tolerate such tactics?

The problem was that he had to choose sides. He was either with the Arabs or he supported the Jews, that's all there was to it. And even then he didn't have the freedom to choose. That was the difference between Phil Matthews and him: the reporter belonged to the world as a whole, his loyalty could be transferred from one group to another, and his choices knew no formal bounds. It wasn't so for people like Moussa. His allegiance had been shaped at birth. He owed his family everything, pure and simple; after that he had his *hamuleh* to consider; and then there were his fellow Palestinians, followed by all Muslims in general. This order was permanent and could not be reversed. As repellent as he found Hamas, he therefore had to cheer them on as they battled the Israelis from house to house in Gaza.

"Here's a question for you. If you were Jewish, what would you do?"

"I'm sorry?"

"Let's say you were Jewish — your name was Avi Greenbaum. Let's say you lived in West Jerusalem and you speak Hebrew. What would you make of the world around you?"

"You mean, what would I think of Moussa Shakir?"

"Yes."

"I don't know. I suppose I would see things from a Jewish perspective and would think like a Jew and act like one, too. My loyalty would be to the Jews and, if I had to choose between the Arabs and my side, the Jews would win out every time. Although some Jews side with us and not Israel. While I appreciate their help, I don't understand their choices."

"So would you be bombing Gaza and arresting Palestinians?"

"Yes. I suppose I would."

"So are the Israelis right to do what they're doing?"

"It doesn't mean they're right. They're pursuing their interests. They are doing what is good for their fellow Jew."

"So should we be condemning them? The world, that is?"

"I don't know. Yes. I mean, I'm glad there are people attached to our cause. It is very rough in Gaza now."

He was smiling to himself. When he was five years old, he'd come across a puddle on Al-Wad Road. This little pool had attracted him because it had reflected perfectly the world above it, the one difference being left and right were reversed. *That tree is to the right of me*, he'd imagined the puddle's Moussa saying, even as he (the real-life Moussa) had countered, *No, it's to my left.* In his mind he'd then switched places with the image and both had agreed that they'd been both right and wrong. But in the puddle the tree *had* been to the right and because the reflection had to to navigate his world, he had to act as if his view were the sound one.

Perhaps realizing that he'd been pushing Moussa, Phil Matthews asked some easier questions, such as how the crisis in Gaza was affecting his family. Moussa explained, without going into details, that the family business was busy now because people were worried and stocking up on food. And visiting his father was out of the question: the prison was off limits until the situation cooled. On a more personal note, Matthews asked about his plans for the summer and who he was rooting for in that night's game, Italy or France. Moussa said he admired Zidane and would be cheering for the French that evening. With the interview on the verge of ending, Phil Matthews asked if Moussa's team would be playing the Israelis soon.

"We're meeting next week," Moussa said. "Unless there are interruptions."

"Interruptions?"

"If the situation worsens, the game might get cancelled. Otherwise the players might roll out of control."

"Maybe that's more of a reason to play: to show both sides you can compete without fighting? I mean, isn't that the purpose of sport?"

"I suppose," Moussa said. But as Phil Matthews wound the interview up, Moussa traded looks with the *Daffawiyya*. The man smiled thinly, as if to say he knew what Moussa was thinking and, yes, he agreed 100 percent. For all his warmth and excellent questions, his boss knew nothing about Jews and Arabs, not if he believed a game of soccer could make a difference in that part of the world. Such thinking was the sign of a deluded idealist.

It was funny, in a sad sort of way. Phil Matthews had to believe this long tunnel had an end, that one day everyone would be like him, friendly and tolerant of everything around him. And, who knows, maybe they would one day.

But only once they'd hammered their foes into submission.

CHAPTER TWENTY-THREE

Avi stepped from his room into the hallway. It was 9:00 a.m. and gorgeous outside. His plan was to eat breakfast with Dan, who had slept at home the night before, after which he would practise his clarinet awhile, and, at eleven, join his team for an hour of drill practice. They had a match scheduled for the following day and it had been a while since they'd played together. At some point, too, he would phone Zohara and arrange to see her later that evening. All in all it would be a great day.

Halfway to the kitchen he paused. Was that cigarettes he smelled? He glanced across the living room to the front door, which was standing open. Dan was outside. He was dressed in his uniform but it wasn't fully buttoned. His hair was uncombed and he was smoking. That was odd. He never smoked this early unless....

"What's wrong?" he asked, joining his brother.

"Where's your shirt?" Dan spoke. Avi hadn't put it on and his brother was a stickler for such things.

"What's wrong?" Avi repeated. "I know something's up."

Dragging on his cigarette, Dan crushed it out and flicked it to the dumpster. He pulled out a pack and lit a second one. The city's sounds intruded: there was a nest nearby, with cheeping birds; a woman telling her kids to wake up; the clatter of a garbage truck further down the street; the hiss of a cat defending its turf; and, from several apartments all at once, the drone of radios and TVs blaring. This last detail increased his suspicions. Why were people tuning into the news?

"There's been an incident," Dan said, from the middle of a cloud.

"In Gaza?"

"No. In Lebanon. Our turf was fired on and two humvees were attacked. Three soldiers were killed and two kidnapped. One tank followed after the aggressors, but was blown up by a mine and more soldiers died."

"This doesn't make sense. We're at peace with Lebanon…."

"Tell that to Hezbollah. They're behind these attacks."

Avi stood in silence as Dan went on. Their troops were going into Lebanon soon, never mind that they were still busy in Gaza. It was too early to say how the crisis would unfold, but the rumour was that the Syrians were stirring and other Arab parties might get involved. All leave had been cancelled within the army. Dan had called his unit commander and was waiting to hear back from him. He might be going to Gaza or north of the border, unless they kept him at his usual post. He would have his answer soon enough.

His brother was calm and speaking in a low tone. Avi understood that he had to suppress his fear, and he was able to do so with surprising ease. He said he would fix them breakfast, scrambled eggs if Dan approved. He ducked inside, leaving Dan to finish his smoke. He went to his room and slipped on a shirt, then hurried to the kitchen and turned on the stove. Two minutes later there were six eggs frying, bread was toasting, and he was fixing a salad. He also had the coffee going — he had mixed it extra strong.

In the midst of these proceedings, the telephone rang. His brother answered and chatted a minute. Avi closed his eyes.

It would never end, would it? Thousands of calls were being placed at that moment and an empty feeling was assaulting people just like him, brothers, parents, and children of soldiers. As these men and women received their orders, civilians would have to sit and wait, praying their relatives would emerge unscathed. Whatever their convictions, whether they were peaceniks or militants, secular or religious, all of them were under the gun just now. If they were going to survive this threat, they would have to do what men must do, regardless of the cost involved. And doubtless when this war was over — and Avi prayed it would finish quickly — it would create further tensions in its wake and light the long wick to yet another explosion. There was no solution. Both conflicts were in regions that the Israelis had abandoned over the last few years, the Gaza Strip and Lebanon. Far from gaining peace as a result, their retreat had led to yet more conflict. So what on earth did the future hold if neither force nor disengagement could lead to peace...?

"The eggs will burn if you don't turn them."

Opening his eyes, Avi smiled at Dan. As his brother set the toast on two plates, Avi turned the stove off and served the eggs. Pouring cups of coffee, he took a seat.

"I have to make this quick."

"You have your orders?"

"They're expecting me up North."

"You'll be fighting up in Lebanon?"

"Not just yet. We'll send in our planes and see what they can do."

Dan smiled and took a bite of the eggs. He had combed his hair, buttoned his shirt, and pulled his uniform into shape. His posture, too, was ramrod straight as if, even while eating, he represented the state; his head was tilted forward, though, to keep himself from spilling on his uniform. He looked confident yet vulnerable; he was a tool of death but could be killed in an instant. His fear tried to assert itself but Avi was too strong.

Dan mentioned Zidane — the French soccer player who had butted an Italian and robbed the French team of their shot at the World Cup. The news was old — it happened a week earlier — but last night the guy had been on TV, explaining his version of events to a talk-show host. Avi listened moodily. He couldn't eat.

"Are you nervous?" he finally asked.

"I feel dazed more than anything. We didn't see this coming, not from Lebanon."

"But there could be serious fighting."

"There'll be fighting all right. But we'll win, more or less, and the violence will die down for now, only to rear its head in future."

"So that's what lies in store for us? Bloody conflicts every few years, and bombs and condemnation from abroad?"

"Your friend Zohara must be getting to you," Dan joked — he had heard all about her left-wing convictions. He consulted his watch and took another bite of egg. As he chewed, he was running through a mental checklist, of stuff he would need besides the obvious equipment, a book, extra socks, sunglasses, chewing gum. And cigarettes. He would need lots and lots of them. There were papers, too, he wanted in good order, the banking, bills, and arrangements for the car (its transmission needed fixing). At the same time he felt he had to address the occasion and that was why he set his cutlery down and eyed Avi with the look of an old soldier.

"I don't know how this war will end, although I'm sure we'll extinguish it more or less. I do know what my own role is. When I'm not in uniform — and this applies to you now — I'll take advantage of the stuff around me and study and work and hang out with my friends. When duty calls, and I'm told I'm needed, I'll follow my orders, without cowardice I hope, but without punching back any more than I have to. I'll be generous when events allow and respect our 'cousins' to the best of my ability. They have to know we're here to stay; but they should know, as well, that we can be good neighbours.

"These are early days yet, you have to remember. The country is less than sixty years old. When the

United States was sixty, it was only half-formed. It was full of violence and really bad ideas — much worse than the ones we live by here. And look at it today. Their true ideals eventually shone through. The same is true of us. Our values are great, and they'll shine through too. A hundred years from now, we'll have security and justice. Or maybe it'll take a hundred years more. The point is, we have to get from here to there. By going about our business, by fighting when we have to, but by remembering that the Arabs deserve a fair shake too, we'll get there, eventually. Until we reach that stage, we have to endure; that's the only possible course of action."

Dan stood and drained his coffee in one swallow. Walking by Avi, he squeezed his shoulder and disappeared into his room. Avi didn't know what to think. He felt so useless, staying behind while his brother fought. Was he supposed to go swimming or play soccer with his friends or practice his clarinet while Dan ran the risk of being blown to pieces? Would he and Zohara sit down to coffee as bullets did their best to kill his brother?

"You haven't touched your eggs," Dan said. He was carrying his gun, cap, and knapsack and was ready to take his place in the ranks. Avi smiled and stood up from the table, intending to escort his brother outside, to the street, to his barracks, to the battlefield even.

"I'm off," Dan said. "And here's what I expect. When *Ima* gets back from work, set her mind at ease — we're men and they're expecting us to show no fear. That's your main priority. And carry on as normal. One day soon you'll be in my position, and in the mean time you should enjoy your routines. It will comfort me to know you're safe and happy. Can you do this?"

Avi nodded. He wasn't scared … he wasn't, but he was fighting desperately to contain his tears.

"Good. Don't use up all my aftershave when you see Zohara." With his free hand he grabbed Avi and squeezed. That was more than Avi could bear. For five, ten seconds the Greenbaum boys embraced, then Dan broke loose and stepped outside. Avi heard him call to a neighbour: figuring that he was off to war, she wished him luck and a safe return. His footsteps faded. The only sign he'd been there earlier was his plate at the table and the smell of cigarettes.

Avi took a seat in Dan's chair. The apartment was silent; as silent as a tomb. It would take him a good hour at least before he could tear himself from this last contact with his brother.

— • —

Moussa was hurrying to the family stall. He'd studied fractals till late the night before and had only woken up at ten that morning. He'd kicked himself because there was stuff to deliver and his brother would be waiting for him to show up.

As he moved along Al-Wad Road, he passed a few people talking in serious tones. He smiled at the ones he knew but they didn't seem to notice. Only a cat glanced his way: as he drew near, it dropped some scraps and darted into a half-open doorway.

On either side of the family stall, knots of men were locked in discussion. Their voices were raised and they were gesturing impatiently. He instinctively knew that something grave had happened, even graver than the events in Gaza. He sprinted the remaining distance to the stall.

"What's happening?" he asked Ahmed, who was sorting through bags and getting orders ready. His movements were unusually calm and Moussa knew he must be angry.

"You were up till late," Ahmed observed, "What were you doing at 2:00 a.m.? I got up for water and saw your light was still on."

"I was reading math. But tell me: what's going on?"

"It's Hezbollah," Mustafa cried, overhearing Moussa's question. "They attacked the Israelis earlier and killed three soldiers and snatched two others. A tank rolled after them but it hit a mine. Imagine that! Hezbollah smashed one of their tanks!"

Others started commenting too: how they didn't really like Hezbollah but they were tough and committed and would burn the Jews' fingers, a fitting price for what was happening in Gaza. Two young men said they yearned to travel North, to help in the campaign against the Israelis, but the roads were hopelessly blocked. Someone said they should riot in Jerusalem and spread the unrest to the West Bank, too, to distract the Jews further and dilute their forces. Someone was singing "Baladi, Baladi" and waving a miniature flag.

But there were other voices, more realistic ones. One man had lots of relatives up North: would they be hit by Hezbollah's missiles? Tourists would stay away all summer and business would suffer as a result: how were merchants going to make it through the winter? The cost of food would mount, and the police might stop them from moving about freely, and riots would ensue, which would lead to violence, and violence to grieving, and grieving to more violence. On and on the cycle would run, and Hezbollah was only making it spin more quickly. Yes, they were tired of living like mice, but do mice band together and tell the cat what to do? What would they win, that was the question. It was all too clear what they were going to lose.

Bit by bit the merchants moved off. Some wore exulted looks, but most seemed worried, as their anger ate at them from deep within.

Moussa stepped inside the stall. Ahmed was readying the orders still and stacking a barrow with goods to deliver. The next few minutes passed in silence and, solely to divert himself, Moussa picked at some sunflower seeds. He could imagine the situation up in Lebanon; it was much like the one over in Gaza: blasts, screams, shots, blood, and lots and lots of people grieving. And how was he responding? What would he do through the length of this crisis? He would wander the streets of the Muslim Quarter, delivering sacks of rice and beans. And when this chore was finished, he would make his way home, he would eat in safety, bathe in safety, study, read, and relax in safety, when hell was breaking loose around him.

There was anger in him now, lots of it, and he was glad it surfaced so easily. But what was he supposed to *do*? What all men do, but what was that?

"What do we do now?" he asked, thrusting aside the sunflowers seeds.

"I will have the barrow ready in a moment," Ahmed answered, glancing up from his store of supplies.

"That's not what I mean. I'm referring to our help-lessness. *Ab* is in prison. They'll come to search our store before long. We're losing in Gaza. We'll lose in Lebanon. I wish, I wish I could somehow act. I wish there was something I could do to help, without strapping a bomb to my chest."

Ahmed stood, stepped over the sacks and sat on an old, sweat-stained chair. He motioned Moussa to sit on a second, creaky stool.

"My preference would be to act as well," he said, helping himself to some roasted almonds. "But I'm not very good at violence, nor do I see the profit it brings. What is Gaza like just now? It is without power and lights and drinking water. The inhabitants are cowering or wandering in a daze, unless they're firing on the Israelis. A hopeless effort but I wish them well. There is nothing gained, that's what I'm saying. This violence will have no positive effect."

"So what do we do?" Moussa cried, rejecting the almonds his brother pushed towards him. "I can't just sit and let my anger devour me."

"I can't answer for everyone. I can only say what I've decided for myself. Our family has been here for genera-tions. Many Shakirs have sat in this stall and done exactly what I do now. I feel their presence and will never leave this place. To the extent that it is possible, I will pass all my days here, opening this stall in summer and winter, and serving every passerby: Arabs, Jews, Christians, tourists. When the police arrive to inspect my papers, I will never give them a reason to expel me, but will smile and cooperate and offer them almonds. And every time our neighbours see me, they will think of me as a familiar landmark, a tree whose roots are sunk so deep that it is impossible to move even one of its branches. And my children will do the same, and their children too.

"We are very good at lingering, we Palestinians. The Jew has had a history of wandering, of clinging to his faith as he was driven about. That was his peculiar genius. Our genius is outlasting those who have entered this land, or, at least absorbing them into our midst. We are flowing with the blood of Egyptians and Greeks and Samaritans and Nabataeans, and other ancient tribes as well. And so, as the Jew passes my stall, he should know that he can't keep us at bay forever, any more than you can defeat the sea with towering walls of brick and concrete. And if they do drive us out, we will wait on the periphery, applying steady pressure through our yearning and numbers. We have been mistreated by many nations; many, indeed, have been much crueler than the Jews. But always we return, in one form or another. This is our talent and it is from this talent that our victory will emerge."

As Moussa listened, he gradually grew calmer. He was starting to see his brother in a different light. While Ahmed had no stomach for heroics, firing guns, or dying in a blaze of glory, there was a quiet power to him. And maybe his vision was the one to follow. While Hamas would live and die by the sword, his brother's steadiness would last forever, would force the enemy to come to terms or cast them into obscurity over many generations, the way the sea or desert always claimed its due.

Without a word, Moussa kissed his brother. He then stood and set his hands on the barrow. War or not, there were deliveries to be made.

CHAPTER TWENTY-FOUR

The day would be a scorcher. It wasn't yet 11:00 a.m. and Avi was soaked with sweat; and they hadn't even started the match. His team was heading to the nearby field where Yossi had told them to meet. He'd met Rami in a nearby café to determine if a final game was worth it. They'd decided it was, so Yossi contacted Avi who in turn had been in touch with the team. No one was eager and who could blame them? Still, they'd gathered at their favourite *makolet* and from there were plodding to the soccer field.

Far from improving, things were getting worse. Hezbollah had been firing missiles by the thousands. While Israeli casualties were low, the North had been evacuated. Citizens were streaming from dozens of towns, Haifa had been emptied — the city was a shadow of itself. The Israelis had been busy with their planes. The IAF had knocked out power in south Lebanon, and destroyed a variety of launching sites and dozens of buildings being used by Hezbollah. According to reports, there were lots and lots of casualties, not just fighters but civilians too. At the same time troops were assembling in the North and preparing to make their way across the border, to stem the flow of rockets that were hitting Jewish soil.

The team walked in silence. Avi wasn't the only one with family involved. Ilan's father had been called North also, Erez's brother was over in Gaza, and Shimshon had family living in Haifa who'd been given the order to leave their homes. Everyone was watching the news, and got truly frightened when the phone started ringing. People were trying to go about their business — Shosh was going into work for example — but they were apprehensive and ready to explode at the slightest provocation.

"Those goddamn Arabs," Ilan said. "We cleared out of Lebanon. What more do they want?"

"It's the same in Gaza," Erez snarled. "We left the area and removed our settlers. What thanks did we get? Missiles and more missiles!"

"We were crazy to leave!" Shimshon agreed. "We

should have known they would use our weakness against us!"

"My dad always says there's one answer," Ilan growled. "An M-16 that's locked and loaded. If the Arabs sense weakness, they'll cut your throat!"

The group continued to talk this way as they marched towards the soccer field. With every step, the sun grew fiercer and more and more of their restraint dissolved. At one point they passed an old, empty lot: junk lay strewn amidst its dried out weeds, wooden planks, broken tiles, rusty pipes, and an old, smashed radio. Without a word Ilan swerved into this field and helped himself to a length of pipe. He swung it and smiled as it whistled through the air. Erez, Shimshon, and the others followed suit, arming themselves with planks and tiles and anything that might serve them well in a fight. Not to be outdone, Avi grabbed the radio. He pulled out its antenna and snapped it off: it was three feet long and vicious-looking. He whipped the air a couple of times: it would leave a lasting mark on his aggressors.

Equipped for a showdown, they headed towards the field again. Their movements seemed synchronized and they could have been mistaken, at a glance, for soldiers.

There wasn't a single word exchanged. The time for talk was over and something else would take place.

— • —

Amir stumbled as he crossed Ha Tzanhanim, en route for the field where the Israelis were waiting. He bumped into Mohammed who collided with Abdul, provoking curses through the chain of players. Someone told Mahmoud to watch his feet, and Mahmoud answered with an insult of his own. Fists might have flown but Amir told them to pipe down. They shouldn't waste their anger; they should save it for the Jews.

The mood was heated. While all of them were delighted that Haifa had been hit, Gaza was still suffering and Arab towns were under fire. Abdul had relatives in al Shaykh Danun, a village five kilometres east of Nahariya. His aunt had told him that a house had been struck and a six-year-old boy had been severely injured. And Mahmoud's family on the outskirts of Tiberias had seen rockets explode in the nearby hills. It was like Hezbollah couldn't tell their friends and enemies apart.

The Palestinians were scared that the Jews would fire all their workers, the Arab ones at least. Over time they would block the roads and isolate towns and prevent people from moving, leading to shortages and a loss of wages. People in the area were starting to hoard.

"It's stupid to be playing," Amir grumbled. "The game is supposed to lead to peace, but look at the Jews. They're masters of violence."

"They bombed five buildings today," Abdul chimed in. "Then they trucked milk and rice into the region, as if hoping that food will bring the dead back to life."

"I hope Hezbollah kicks their ass," Amir said, "and teaches them the meaning of death."

"We got a note about my brother," Mahmoud cried. "They're putting him in prison for at least two years, because he punched a soldier who was pushing him around."

They continued speaking as they muscled forward, every statement adding fuel to their rage. Amir said they had to do something; he repeated this over and over again. When they wandered by a construction site, he plunged straight into it and rummaged about. Planks and rods were strewn all over, as well as piles and piles of stones. Amir filled his pockets with these, then hefted a solid-looking two-by-four. Impressed by his example, the others wandered around the lot and armed themselves with an array of weapons; Moussa found a hammer some worker had forgotten. It had a rubber grip and its heavy mass was reassuring. These tools, if incautiously handled, could cause serious damage. But that was the point: they wanted to cause harm. Harm was good. Harm was holy. They would beat the Jews until their bones cracked open and they begged for mercy and dyed the earth red.

Girded for battle, they hurried forward, their expressions as hard as the stones in their pockets.

The sun was bright and searingly hot. The cat was growling in satisfaction. In a dumpster just beside a field it had stumbled on a chicken leg, thick with meat and grease and fat. It had dragged this haul into the middle of the field, to prevent a rival from muscling in, where it was ripping off large chunks of flesh and bolting them fiercely. It had managed five large mouthfuls already and it wasn't even halfway through, a good thing too as the Siamese was starving.

The cat was startled by a movement to its right. Jumping just in time, it dodged a stone from out of nowhere.

There were shouts of rage and more stones fell. Humans were advancing on both sides. They were running hard and brandishing sticks and practically tearing the air with their screams. The cat looked long and hard at the meat. This wasn't fair. It wasn't every day such food came along and now they wanted to take it away. Should it seize the bone and scamper off, or try to grab a mouthful more? Another stone went whistling by. The thickset humans were lumbering closer.

Growling bitterly it took to its heels. An instant later the humans came running, gasping and shouting and still throwing stones. The two groups were dangerously close and each human was facing a chosen opponent. All of them were about to pounce — the cat was a fighter and could sense these things — when two deep voices brought them to a stop.

Two more humans had arrived on the scene. They were bigger and older than everyone else, and the white one's arm was wounded. They were angry with the smaller ones, and yet (was it the cat's imagination) they were scared of them, too. Each was trying to lead his group away, by threatening them, yes, but by cajoling them too — this was the sort of trick a big weak cat will practise on its juniors.

The Siamese perked up its ears. The groups were moving off. They weren't shouting now and their sticks had been lowered. So maybe it could fetch that meat after all…!

One of the humans slipped on the chicken! He hadn't watched where he was stepping and the meat was slippery with delicious grease and fat and he had skidded on it and crashed to the ground.

The other group was making noises. It was a terrible sound — *ha ha ha* —and the cat could tell they were sounding a challenge. Sure enough, their rivals were turning. There were yells again. Both sides were grimacing and charging now. The bigger ones were intervening but ... something hit the wounded one. He stooped forward, his hands on his skull. His big friend was helping him but ... he was struck as well.

The cat licked its lips.

The others were fighting. The cat liked fighting. There were gasps and groans and snarls of fury. Their heavy limbs were everywhere and they were on each other and hitting and kicking. A few were swinging objects. Some were losing blood and screaming in pain, or maddened fury. One was down and didn't seem to be moving. Another.... A stone sailed close and sent the cat running.

It stopped when it reached the old stone tower. Cowering in its doorway it was studying two more humans. One was holding a rusted hammer, the other a shiny metal stick. They were facing each other and practically spitting. Each one's face was difficult to read. It could have been distorted with rage but there might have been something else as well. Something only humans have. But if that were so why were they confronting each other? Why was one swinging his hammer about, while the other kept whipping and whipping the air? They weren't friends. The rest were fighting. It was up to them to fight as well.

And they knew it. They knew that they should be fighting. And they intended to, the cat could see. That's why they weren't backing off. They weren't closing in but they weren't backing off. And each kept shaking and swinging his weapon and screaming to work his bloodlust up. Their faces were hard. Beneath that surface softness they were stone cold hard. When would they fight? *Go on, fight!* the Siamese growled.

It settled itself. It was prepared to wait. It might take ages but, like everyone else, they would soak the earth with their blood, wouldn't they?

GLOSSARY

HEBREW

Abba — dad

Aliyah — move to Israel

Chablan Mishtara — bomb disposal unit

Eretz Yisrael — the land of Israel

Galut — the diaspora; the world outside Israel

Giveret — "lady," a respectful term of address

Golani — an elite fighting unit in the Israeli army

Hakol beseder — everything's okay

Haredim — the ultra-orthodox Jews

Hatikvah — the Israeli national anthem

Ima — mom

Kibbutznik — someone who lives on a *kibbutz* (an Israeli collective community)

Kol hakevod — well done

Kotel — the only wall that survives the Jews' Second Temple (which was destroyed by the Romans in 70 C.E.)

L'chaim — "to life"; said when making a toast

Makolet — small, corner grocery store

Malkosh — the last rain of spring (there is almost always no rain in Israel during the summer)

Mazel tov — congratulations

Mensch — a decent person

Midrachov — a pedestrian mall

Moshav — cooperative agricultural community with individual farms

Motek — term of affection, "sweetie"

Pesach — the Hebrew word for Passover

Shabbat — Saturday, a day of rest in Israel

Shabbat shalom — greeting, "have a peaceful Shabbat"

Shesh besh — backgammon

Shin Bet — Israel's internal security and intelligence service

Shwarma — meat shaved from a spit and served in pita bread

Stachim — the occupied territories

Streimel — a fur hat worn by married, ultra-Orthodox men

Shtetl — a type of small, Eastern European town where many Jews once lived

Teudat oleh — Immigration card or certificate

Teudat zehut — identity card (to be carried at all times by Israeli adults)

Torah — the five books of Moses and the cornerstone of Jewish law and religion

Tzahal — acronym meaning literally "Defense Army for Israel"; the Israeli armed forces

Yeshiva — Jewish religious school

Yom Hashoah — Holocaust remembrance day

Zaidy — granddad

ARABIC

Ab — dad

As salamu alaykum — greeting used when bidding people welcome

Alhamdulilah — praise be to God; equivalent of "halleluyah"

Daffawiya — a native of the West Bank

Eid al Fitr — holiday marking the end of Ramadan (and the breaking of the fasting period)

Foules — cooked fava beans, a staple food of the Middle East

Gazazweh — native of Gaza

Habibi — term of affection, "dear," "darling"

Hamas — an acronym for "Islamic Resistance

Movement"; its members are deeply religious, govern the Gaza Strip and are prepared to use violence to oust Israelis from the *stachim* (and possibly Israel itself).

Hamuleh — collective noun used for extended family (aunts, uncles, cousins etc.)

Halawa — Middle Eastern confectionery

Insha'Allah — "if Allah wills"; similar to the English "God willing"

Irdh — honour

Jadda — grandma

Keffiyeh — traditional check-patterned Palestinian head-dress

Kunafa — a Middle Eastern dessert

Nakba — the "catastrophe"; i.e. the creation of the state of Israel and the consequent loss of land and independence for Palestinians

Sada — a strong, bitter coffee

Shaheed — a term meaning "witness" or "martyr" and applied to Muslims who sacrificed themselves out of religious conviction; it is often applied to suicide bombers

Sharia — strict Islamic law

Shebab — "young men," the young Palestinians who fight the Israelis

Shuk — marketplace

Ta'alaa — Almighty

Teita — grandma

Thobes — traditional ankle-length robe with long
sleeves

Um — mom

Ya'allah — Dear God (an exclamation)

ALSO BY NICHOLAS MAES

Laughing Wolf
978-1-55488-385-1
$12.99

It is the year 2213. Fifteen-year-old Felix Taylor is the last person on Earth who can speak and read Latin. In a world where technology has defeated war, crime, poverty, and famine, and time travel exists as a distinct possibility, Felix's language skills and knowledge seem out of place and irrelevant. But are they?

A mysterious plague has broken out. Scientists can't stop its advance, and humanity is suddenly poised on the brink of eradication. The only possible cure is *lupus ridens*, or Laughing Wolf, a flower once common in ancient Rome but extinct for more than 2,000 years.

Felix must travel back to Roman times, circa 71 B.C., to retrieve the flower. But can he navigate through the dangers and challenges of the world of Spartacus, Pompey, Cicero? And will he find the Laughing Wolf in time to save his how family and everyone else from the Plague of Plagues?

Locksmith
978-1-55002-791-4
$11.99

Twelve-year-old Lewis Castorman is a master locksmith: there is no lock on earth that he is unable to open. He is therefore flattered when world-renowned chemist Ernst K. Grumpel invites him to his office in New York City and offers him a lock-picking assignment. His confidence quickly turns to dismay, however, when he learns this job will take him to Yellow Swamp in northern Alberta, the scene of a disastrous chemical spill a year earlier. He is also horrified to discover that Grumpel is utterly ruthless and, through his chemical inventions, can alter the rules of nature at his will. But the assignment is one that Lewis can't refuse.

How is Grumpel able to create such miraculous transformations? What secrets has he locked away and why has he taken pains to store them in Alberta? Despite the strange discoveries Lewis will make at every turn in his adventures, nothing will prepare him for the final encounter that awaits him in Yellow Swamp.

Available at your favourite bookseller.

DUNDURN PRESS
www.dundurn.com

What did you think of this book?
Visit www.dundurn.com
for reviews, videos, updates, and more!

CPSIA information can be obtained
at www.ICGtesting.com
Printed in the USA
BVHW08s0808170918
527707BV00022B/705/P

9 781554 887972